Saskia Walker

Saskia Walker is one of the top erotic writers of the millennium.
~Author, Alison Tyler

Saskia Walker's vivid writing is redolent with a lush, simmering sensuality that winds around its joyous romantic heart.
~Author, Portia Da Costa

Total-E-Bound Publishing books by Saskia Walker:

Play for Today
Winner Takes All
Brits in Time: Brazen Behaviour
Running Wild
One Enchanted Night
The Right Men for the Job

INESCAPABLE

SASKIA WALKER

Inescapable
ISBN # 978-0-85715-060-8
©Copyright Saskia Walker 2010
Cover Art by April Martinez ©Copyright 2010
Interior text design by Claire Siemaszkiewicz
Total-E-Bound Publishing

Published in 2010 by Total-E-Bound Publishing, Think Tank, Ruston Way, Lincoln, LN6 7FL, United Kingdom.

Manufactured in the USA.

INESCAPABLE

Dedication

For Mark, always.

Chapter One

How badly do you want it?
How badly do you want to come?

When those words appeared on her computer screen Lily's pulse raced erratically, anticipation gathering inside her. In that moment nothing else existed — not her day job or the bills or these cold winter nights — because Lily Howard was having an intense virtual affair with a man she only knew as A.W.

If I were there with you now I would ask you to pull your skirt up for me, and I'd ask you to do it nice and slow...

Lily exhaled. Her hands automatically went to the hem of her skirt, fingers teasing along the edge of it, ready to pull it up. She savoured the anticipation for a moment, her thoughts entirely in tune with the mystery online lover who had set her libido on fire. Then she shuffled her skirt up her thighs and rocked her hips back and forth as she eased it up. Stroking her hands over her bare thighs, she sighed aloud, before quickly touching the keyboard again, her right hand moving over the mouse sensuously, as if she could maintain contact with her virtual lover through that action alone.

...and then I'd put my hands between your knees and push your legs apart. You'd like that, wouldn't you? I think I know you well enough now, L.

"Oh yes, you certainly do," she murmured, spellbound by the connection they had developed. Trembling as she traced her fingertips over the keyboard, she wished it were him that she were touching — wished that she could rest her hand over his as he caressed her body. Slowly, she typed her response.

Yes, I would like that.

As his reply appeared on her screen, her clothes began to feel tight and restrictive, her breath trapped in her lungs.

I'm thinking about what you told me last night...I'd like to see you do that.

A shiver ran down her spine, her entire skin kindling. She rested her elbows on the desk, briefly covering her eyes with her hands. She'd let go the night before — she'd confessed fantasies she hadn't even consciously admitted to herself before then. It had made her feel so good, sharing her secrets with someone who wanted to know, a man who told her he got hard in response to her deepest fantasies and cravings. The only man she'd ever actually confessed these things to in person had laughed at her. Not A.W., and she'd felt validated by his reaction.

Oblivious to the encroaching evening outside her bedroom window, her hips rocked back and forth on her chair, her pussy on fire, her core clenching with need. When she looked back at the screen, she saw that he was typing again. She was wound up tight, ready to let loose, and he seemed determined to tease her. Usually there was more back and forth in their chat, but he seemed particularly focused tonight.

I want you to touch yourself now, touch yourself and make yourself come. Do it for me.

"Oh, please," she muttered aloud. Physical need had her firmly in its grip. With restless fingers she swiped away the damp heat gathering in her cleavage. This is how it had been every evening since they'd hooked up. A.W. had invited her to join him in a private chat room, two faceless strangers confessing their most erotic fantasies in torrid exchanges that ended in mutual climax. Resistance only heightened her awareness of how much she wanted it, the interactions revealing how lewd she could really get, given any encouragement.

Pushing back, she rested one stacked heel up against the edge of the desk. With the light from the screen falling over her open legs, it felt almost as if he was right there standing between her thighs, telling her to touch herself and watching her as she masturbated for him. Her head dropped back, her eyes squeezing shut for a moment before she looked back at her PC.

With her shirt open, she already had her bra cups pulled down so that she could touch her breasts, her skirt up around her hips. Running one needy hand over her up-tilted breasts, the other moved between her thighs and under her G-string, where she was hot and damp. With one hand locked over her pussy, her face heated as she pushed one finger inside. Keeping her eyes fixed on the computer screen she watched as his next message appeared.

How close are you to coming? Tell me, so that I can picture it.

Moaning softly, she swung from side to side in her swivel chair.

Or are you too close to type…?

"Tease," she whispered, a breathless laugh escaping her. Her hand was slick and she was totally unable to break away to respond. Her silence was admittance though, and it made her outrageously horny. Wired, she squirmed on her hand, her face heating. His next message came fast. He liked to push her over the edge, to be the one who made her climax.

I would so like to be there, watching you while you make yourself come.

The suggestion of being watched by him—being told what to do by him—pushed her ever closer to orgasm. He knew it would, it was one of the things that she had confessed to him. Squirming on the hand wedged between her thighs, her clit throbbed as she rubbed her palm over it, wave after wave of pleasure emanating from that point. Dropping back in her chair, she pictured him watching her, right now, a dark mystery man who pushed her to her limits. Her body writhed and she spasmed, clenched, then released, a lighting strike of pleasure spearing out across every nerve ending in her groin, spiralling out as far as her nipples and her throat, where she burned. A cry of release escaped her open mouth.

Even as she let out that cry and the tension in her body slowly ebbed away, a new message appeared on the screen.

I want to meet you, L. I want to meet you for real.

At first she thought she'd imagined it. She stared at the screen in disbelief, her chest rising and falling in the aftermath of her climax, her breath catching in her throat. Rereading the words, she took it in. Her virtual lover had typed something he had never typed before, not in all the time they had been meeting in the private chat room and getting each other off via this virtual relationship.

Thoughts crowded her mind. To meet him, for real? Unsettling, and yet... Every nerve ending in her body was telling her to say yes, but at the very same time caution was foremost in her mind. She knew nothing about this man, not even his full name. At first she'd liked that ambiguity. The only thing she did know was that he worked in the city. That could mean anything, but she revelled in the mystery surrounding her virtual lover. He could be any man she saw in the street, and yet he was there at the end of the line, for her. She stood up and walked away, suddenly needing space to think.

In the bathroom she turned on the tap and quickly splashed her face with cold water. She pushed back her hair and peered at herself in the mirror. Her eyes were bright and strangely luminous, the colour in her cheeks high. Her thick, dark hair was fuzzed where she had mussed it. She looked as if she'd had sex, real sex. Her virtual lover had been so direct today, so insistent, like he was fired up even more than usual by their exchanges. Then he'd issued the invitation to make it real.

Glancing back through the open door, she could see the computer screen. She had her doubts, but could she resist? It beckoned to her, even now. If it was just the immediate thrill, why did she want to know what he said next? She had to face it, she did want more.

Grabbing the towel, she dried her hands and then walked back to her room, closing the door behind her. Sitting down, she wheeled her chair back towards the desk, quickly reading the words that had appeared on the screen while she'd been gone.

It's been three months now, aren't you curious?
I am.

She touched the edge of the keyboard with trembling fingers, her pulse racing as she considered what to reply. When they'd met in an online dating forum he'd been direct about chatting privately, and the needs they shared. He hadn't forced the issue of who and what she was. Instead he had suggested they take it to a private chat room, which made her think it was just about this, the sexual kick of an online affair, not a real meet. After that, he'd quickly keyed into her sexuality, and her secret desire to be sexually mastered, and watched.

Sitting at the small desk in her tiny bedroom every evening, illuminated only by the computer screen, she thrilled at the secret sexual connection. The medium allowed her to abandon her inhibitions, to say things about her desires and her fantasies that she had never said before. She'd also learnt a lot about the male sexual psyche from A.W., as he teasingly informed her about his responses to her confessions. It was the perfect mutual pleasure exchange. No strings, no complications, and a whole heap of physical rewards.

She'd thought about meeting him, alone in her bed, in her fantasies. But to really meet him—to go on a blind date with a man she'd never seen, but who knew her every sexual fantasy? That was a whole new situation, one weighted with implication, one that she wasn't quite sure she was ready for. It was risky. Even so, a question echoed at the back of Lily's mind, one that always appeared when she was indecisive: *would I regret it if I didn't do it?*

That kind of regret was something she never wanted to live with, regret for *not* having done something. Regret for messing up was somehow easier to accept, but the 'what ifs?' of this life really got to Lily Howard, and she knew this situation would, too, if she didn't take the chance. Trembling, she began to type.

> *Hell, yes, I'm curious. But we risk losing this relationship if we meet. This is so good. What if we didn't have the same sort of connection if we met, like…in the flesh?*

A smiling icon appeared.

In the flesh...sounds good...

She smiled to herself. He was making her warm and fuzzy again. Was that a good thing? They had chatted about more than sex, and they seemed to click. They knew they shared the same favourite pizza topping, and they both preferred action movies over art house. She typed her response quickly, still amused.

Stick with the question that you asked!

She sat back in her chair, more settled as she waited for his response, her mind whirring quickly over the prospect of an actual meet.

Okay, yes, it is a risk, but life is short. Consider this...it might be even better, "in the flesh", as you so enticingly put it.

The man had something. She was about to respond when she sensed that he was going to say more. She was right. She clasped her hands together, feeling both nervous and eager, and then she saw his chat icon flashing again.

Look, I have a confession. My secretary told me I should get out more, meet more women. It made me think, but what it made me think about was you.

Lily gave a soft laugh as she typed her response.

Maybe your secretary has a crush on you. She could have been hinting.

I don't think so. She's married and has five grandchildren. Besides, she's not my type, whereas you are.

How can you know that for sure?

As she waited and watched, she thought about the fact that he had a secretary who was a grandmother. She didn't know that about him. What else didn't she know about this man? A lot. The only thing she did know was that they clicked in some way. Sexually, and maybe even a bit emotionally, too. She felt somehow attuned to him. Was it possible to do that, to feel that way about someone without knowing what they looked like or what they were like to be around? After a lot of thought, she'd decided it was.

L, every time I even see a computer it's you that I think about. It's you who gives me a hard-on at the most inappropriate of times.

She shook her head. His sense of humour had drawn her to him. That and his directness when it came to chatting about sex. He made her feel naughty and sexualised in all the right ways. She typed.

It's the same for me, now. I don't go to the other chat sites anymore.

She'd often considered the fact that he might be doing this with a ton of women, or worse still that he might be married and he shouldn't even be doing this. But would he risk meeting her if he was? Maybe, who could say?

You're the only one I chat to, L. What does it stand for? Lucy? Linda? Laidbacklady?
Seriously, there isn't anyone else like you...you get my attention away from my work. Believe me, that doesn't happen very often. Please think about meeting me.

Laidbacklady. That so wasn't her, no way. The misnomer sent a doubt through her. Then she reminded herself how she felt when she was alone, after their chats. Oh, how she hated switching the PC off, how she hated becoming aware of the sounds of London outside her window and the empty place beside her in bed at night.

She glanced around her bedroom, her mind flitting over the basic facts of her life — the start-up business and tiny flat that she shared with her friend, Andrea. Aside from the Sandwich Boutique and her family and friends, this virtual relationship was her main focus. In fact it had occupied her mind so much lately it had become a major preoccupation.

How would it feel if it were real, if it was something tangible and complete, a real partner to adventure with? Being with someone who helped her peel back the layers of her inhibitions so easily had immense appeal, and for a few short seconds she found her mind running to the possibility of a proper relationship with depth, something to build on. No, she couldn't go into it thinking that — hoping for it. It had to be about fun, nothing else. No expectations of anything more, and no regrets if it didn't work out. That's what it had been about in the virtual world, and she had to meet him with the same attitude.

Meet him. A shiver ran down her spine, and it was a shiver of the excitement. What would it be like, after she had already stripped herself bare for him? There would be no turning away from their sexual connection, no denial, and if it worked under those terms...oh boy. The scent of her arousal hung in the air, a reminder of everything this relationship had already given her.

He was typing again.

> *You haven't said no, and you haven't logged out. I'm reading that as a good sign. Are you interested?*

She couldn't deny it, so she didn't respond. Indecision swamped her, the allure of his invitation vying with her concerns. It was as if she was poised on a precipice and she could scarcely breathe for fear of taking the wrong step. Before she had a chance to reply he was typing again.

> *We can meet in a public place; you don't need to be worried about that.*

A public place would be good. She appreciated his sensitivity on that point. She was wary, very. She'd be stupid not to be, but he was edging it forward all the time. He was so keen. The lure of adventure beckoned to her all the while, and even though her fingers felt strangely immobile, she forced herself through it. She had to make the move, had to take the chance. With her pulse racing and an oddly delirious feeling, she typed the words needed to move it forward.

My name is Lily, and yes, I do want to meet you.

* * * *

When Adrian Walsh closed down his Internet connection, over half an hour later, he sat back in his office chair and said her name aloud.

"Lily." It had a distinctly feminine and yet wistful sound and that reflected his impression of her. He'd played in the chat rooms before. It was like sport to him, nothing serious. The quick get-off, the sexy distraction that was right there at his fingertips after a long day in the office. He didn't really care who he chatted with, he just enjoyed the anonymity of chatting about sex on line.

Then L had captured his attention in a different way. Her words had conveyed each breathless self-discovery as she unfolded herself and her fantasies to him. Perhaps he was more of a voyeur than he'd realised, he thought, wryly mused. Mostly he felt that it was special. The way she'd expressed herself, it didn't seem like she did that all the time. But maybe she did, and he was flattering himself.

Meeting might be a disaster, but what was life without a few risks?

He'd tried to put at her ease by inviting her to his office for their initial meet. A public place showed he had nothing to hide. He wanted her to be chilled with the set up, or she might not even turn up. The need to find out what she was really like had a hold of him these past few days, and he'd felt the urge to edge it forward. She'd bitten. Not immediately, but he'd have put money on the fact she would, eventually.

He smiled to himself and glanced over the paperwork on his desk. The smile quickly faded. The other main thing occupying his mind confronted him, the Carlisle account. He lifted his notes from the front of the file, then sighed and put them down again. He stood up, walking over to the window that looked out over London's business district.

The January sky was ominous, laden with cloud. The city streetlights illuminated it oddly. He'd been here in his own offices a year, and he was doing well. But now he was in a corner. He'd made a stupid, uninformed agreement when he'd taken on this client. Carlisle was wealthy, and he'd offered him incentives to 'tidy up' his accounts. Adrian had done something similar for an associate, Carlisle had said. Well, yes, he'd worked figures favourably to avoid the taxman for another client, but this was altogether different, and it was way out of his league.

He'd foolishly agreed to the terms, without asking around about Carlisle's business interests. Now he knew why the incentive had looked so juicy. It wasn't just that Carlisle wanted a rush job. Something was badly wrong there, and he wished he'd never touched it.

He'd been over-ambitious, taken on a dodgy client without thinking it through, and now his conscience wouldn't let him go ahead. Damn Catholic upbringing, it always seemed to force him to do the right thing. He didn't like feeling trapped and he knew that he was going to have to do something about it. There was only one option, to turn the file over to the police. Even if it meant hellfire rained down on his head, which—judging from what he'd discovered in the paperwork—was quite possible.

He'd been brooding over it when Lily logged in that evening and she'd been a very welcome distraction. But now she was gone and Adrian had to face up to it. He had to go to the police, whether he liked it or not.

Chapter Two

The elevator jolted to a halt. When the doors slid open, Lily's stomach flipped. Her legs felt weak. Five days she'd had to get used to the idea of meeting Adrian, and yet her emotions were all over the place. Her more animal instincts had kept her anticipation at a constant high, fuelled by the idea of live action instead of anonymous stimulation. At the same time, she couldn't quite believe she would soon be face to face with the man she'd been having a virtual sexual relationship with. The two opposing reactions had her in a state of turmoil.

The day had finally dawned and she'd made it this far. She'd even braved the slush-covered January streets in a fancy outfit and heels to meet Mr. Adrian Walsh at his office.

She moved, bumping into the only other occupant of the elevator, a man who was trying to leave at the same time as she was. He was tall, and his fair hair flashed out as he shot her an annoyed look, cold blue eyes scanning her.

"Sorry," she said, and paused as he pushed past her and exited, turning immediately left. People jostled into the elevator, office workers intent on leaving the building at the end of the day. One of the women put her hand on a button on the panel and kept it there while the others piled in. Jolting into action, Lily squeezed through the crowd and hurried out into the corridor.

Facing her was a large stainless steel board mounted on the wall. It listed the occupants of the suites on the 16th floor. Glancing left and right, she noticed how up-market the place was. Polished marble tiles ran the length of the corridor, inscribed steel plaques gleaming on the doors. She still couldn't believe that he was an accountant, a man with his own suite of offices in the heart of London. He'd suggested meeting here, assuring her this was a busy place and there were lots of other people around, which there were. Adrian clearly had a reputation to keep, which was also reassuring.

Scanning the board, she smoothed down the close fitting top and skirt that her flat mate, Andrea, had insisted she borrow, and pulled her thigh-length leather coat closer around her.

Adrian's office was in Suite 16K. The sign indicated that she should turn left. She took a deep breath and forced herself in that direction, resisting the urge to go back to the elevator and disappear into the departing crowd. She wanted to know; she had to find out. If it didn't work…her stomach tightened at the idea of it. It would be awkward, especially after all that they had revealed to each other. That was the worst part.

Glancing at the various company names as she passed the offices, she estimated Suite 16K was the last door on the right. The rude man from the elevator was ahead of her, and he seemed to be headed in the same direction.

Her footsteps slowed.

What if that was him? What if the man with the cold blue eyes was Adrian? Just as the thought occurred to her, the man glanced back over his shoulder and looked directly at her, his eyes narrowing.

He was built large and brutish, and dressed in dark clothing. She didn't think he looked like an accountant. Adrian's easy, sexy, and direct chat had reminded her of a barman she'd met on holiday, the sort of bloke who put women at their ease immediately. That was how she had been picturing him, working a bar in the city. She'd never have guessed he was an accountant. What did an accountant even look like, anyway? She hadn't a clue. Andrea's aunt did their paperwork for the Sandwich Boutique.

The sudden wave of uncertainty sent a shiver through her. The man ahead was moving quickly and had passed the last door on the corridor. That was weird. Where was he going? As she gained on him she felt increasingly uneasy. Drawing to a halt, she paused outside a random door. Perhaps he was lurking around to check her out as she arrived. If it turned out that he was Adrian, she wasn't sure she wanted to go ahead with the date. He had a cold look about him that creeped her out.

What the hell was she getting into, she thought, feeling panicked. When the man turned back again she looked away and put her hand on a door handle for suite 16J, grappling for cover while she cautiously watched him from the periphery of her vision.

With one last glance back over his shoulder, the man stepped over to the window at the end of the corridor, opened it, and climbed out onto the fire escape.

Maintenance man, not accountant.

Lily shook her head and laughed at herself, which released a heap of tension. Then, with a deep, steadying intake of breath, she walked along the corridor to the door of suite 16K. The polished plaque mounted on the door read:

Adrian Walsh, large business accountancy.

She was in the right place. That was a good start. She glanced at her watch. Just a minute or so early, which gave her enough time for her final self-brief. She'd been through it a hundred times, and it did calm her.

They'd agreed on terms. If they didn't click, they could go their separate ways. No big deal. If they did hit it off, they'd already broken through the barriers and a hot, fulfilling sexual relationship awaited, at the very least. Yes, and her body clamoured at the thought of it, her anticipation rising. She adjusted her hair, flicking it back over her shoulders, and then steeled herself and knocked on the door.

Too late to run away, you've done it now.

A cold draught from the open window at the end of the corridor blew over her, wrapping itself around her ankles and making her shiver. She pulled her coat closer, and then crossed her fingers, swallowing hard. "Please let the chemistry be there," she whispered, staring at the door. "Please let him be," she swallowed again, "okay."

* * * *

24

Witness Protection Officer, Seth Jones, stood up as soon as he heard the knock on the door. Instinctively, he reached inside his jacket, resting his hand over the butt of his gun. "Were you expecting anyone?"

Adrian Walsh sat forward in his seat, eyes barely focused on the mid-distance. He shook his head, looking at the door to the corridor with a frown. "I don't think so. Christ, so much has gone on these last two days." He started pushing paperwork around on the desk. "I should have asked Cassandra before I told her to go, but I'm not thinking straight. Her diary is here somewhere."

Seth nodded. This intrusion, whatever it was, might work to his advantage. If unexpected callers unnerved Adrian, he might agree to go into safe housing. "This is exactly why we need to take you into witness protection. Eric Carlisle is a powerful man. He could have one of his men come around here at any time."

Walsh pursed his lips, still looking at his desk as if he didn't want to acknowledge what Seth had just said. He'd been resisting the concept of going into hiding for the past hour, and he was still far from being convinced.

"Okay," Walsh stated, "so Carlisle is a criminal, but I can't believe he'd send someone after me." He threw up his hands in a gesture somewhere between annoyance and despair. "I mean, how could he? He's locked up now, isn't he?"

"Yes, he's in custody, but he'll be highly motivated by the need to stay out of prison in the long term. He has contacts who might think they can persuade you not to give your evidence in court."

Walsh shook his head in disbelief. "I can't afford to go into hiding, my business, my life…"

It was often this way with witnesses who were outsiders to the crime; those who had no idea what the people they were dealing with were actually capable of. Adrian's evidence relied solely on paperwork; figures related to illegal overseas exports that shouldn't have crossed his desk in the first place. Luckily for the police, they had. Carlisle had been sloppy. It was vital information, and Carlisle's associates might want Adrian Walsh out of the picture altogether. That was what Seth was here to prevent. Witness protection was his trade.

There was another knock at the door, and it was more insistent this time. Seth gestured into the adjacent office. "You go in there. Stay out of view. I'll take care of it."

Adrian nodded vaguely and wandered into the office next door. Seth waited until he was out of sight and then headed over to the external door, hand inside his jacket. Senses honed, he opened the door.

Whatever he'd been expecting, it wasn't an attractive woman looking up at him expectantly. She looked soft and somehow vulnerable, and his first response was the urge to stroke her. It was the serious expression in her brown eyes. She was staring at him as if her life depended on him opening the door. Dark hair scrolled over her shoulder, and she had full lips that made him think of sex. Just as he was about to ask if she were lost, her eyes flashed in recognition and that sexy mouth of hers moved into a big smile.

Had they met before? He didn't recognise her, but he met a lot of people. Bemused, Seth lifted an eyebrow in query, resting one hand up against the doorframe and returning her smile.

"Well, hello," she whispered. Sliding one hand inside her coat, she rested it on her hip, provocatively. "So, do you like what you see?"

"I'd be lying if I said I didn't." He couldn't resist, and as he surveyed the rest of the packaging he rued the fact he was on the job. Underneath the coat, she had on a low cut top that bared her midriff, and a short skirt. She had killer curves, a body made for sex. Glossy black heels and sheer stockings emphasised her shapely legs, and a scarf around her throat drew his attention back to the pale skin of her collarbone and cleavage.

She was also giving him a once-over appraisal with a breed of intimacy he wasn't familiar with. Something about his face and his stature—and most probably his occupation—turned women into simpering ninnies around him, and he hated that.

She wasn't waiting to be invited in. Closing the space between them, the soft kitten look had been replaced by something much more focused, and for some reason the situation reminded him of the time his friends had clubbed together for a stripper on his thirtieth birthday. Except this woman was classy, and she was a stunner.

"I'm beginning to wish I'd knocked on your door long before now." Looking up, she flashed him a suggestive glance that hit him right below the belt. Resting one shoulder up against the doorframe, she leant in against him, right next to his chest.

They were barely three inches apart, and she smelled so good. Her dark eyes flashed with mischievous suggestion. His body responded, and his mind played along. He could just picture her on her back, naked, and with him over her. Something about the way she was looking at him set the thoughts loose in his head, as if she were thinking about it, too. She was an invitation on legs, and he was ready to party.

Even so, something about the setup struck him oddly, and whatever it was niggled at the back of his mind as he enjoyed the view. *There's a red-hot woman standing out here, giving you the come on? It's odd.*

She seemed intent on distracting him—she could be looking for someone else, or she could be covering for someone else. He had to stay sharp.

She reached up and slid one hand around his neck, pushing her fingers into his hair. Standing on tiptoe, she brushed her lips over his cheek, breathing him in appreciatively.

Focus Seth, you're on the job. Snatching at her hip as she sidled up against him, he grabbed hold of her and gave the corridor a quick reconnaissance over her shoulder.

She had other ideas. Her hands had dropped to his belt, which she tugged on. "I'm so glad this is real," she whispered, her breath warm on his face.

Real? No, decidedly surreal, Seth thought, as she kissed him and that soft mouth opened under his. His blood was pumping southward ever faster, but his suspicion was also rising. A door slammed. He walked her back against the opposite wall in the corridor, eyes opening. With his hands either side of her head, he pinned her in place and scanned the corridor. There were people emerging from offices at the far end. She didn't even seem to be aware of them, or she didn't care. Instead, she took advantage of her caged position and writhed her body against his, her hands on his hips.

When she moved one knee up the outside of his thigh, he groaned aloud, shooting her a warning glance, his cock alert and eager to be buried inside her.

"Now wait up, missy."

"Why? You said it yourself. If the chemistry is there for us we don't have to wait." She gave a gentle laugh, eyes sparkling, and rested one hand over the bulge in his pants, embracing his cock. "And the chemistry is definitely here for us, wouldn't you say?"

Whoever the hell she was, she was clearly playing the game without a full deck of cards. But her words barely touched him, because the nerves on his back were wired. Something was wrong here, and it wasn't just to do with Miss Hotpants.

Focus, Seth.

Pulling away, he turned to look down the corridor. The fact that her body was warm had highlighted the contrast. Cold air was filling the corridor. The window was open; he could see the fire escape. The window hadn't been open when he arrived. His radar was up.

"Did you open that window?" He grasped the woman by her shoulder.

She frowned. "No, a blond bloke did, he went out there a minute ago."

Shit. It was an old building, a conversion. At this end of the corridor it was likely that the fire escape went around the outside of these offices. He moved fast, dragging the woman with him as he headed back to his mark.

A split second later the sound of breaking glass reached him, followed by a shot ringing out. Seth cursed aloud. The woman cried out.

Was she a decoy?

He hauled her inside the office, registering the shock and confusion in her eyes as he did so. His gut instinct was that she didn't know what was going on, but he couldn't be sure. He shut the door and pushed her to the ground.

"Stay down." He put his finger to his lips, resting one foot against her side to keep her from getting up.

"But..." Startled, she stared up at the gun in his hand with wide eyes.

Craning his neck, he caught sight of movement in the adjacent office and saw Adrian's hand reaching up for the edge of the desk. He was down on the floor, but thankfully he was still moving.

I should have been in there.

I should be in there now.

Glancing back at the woman to make sure she stayed where she was, he was momentarily halted in his tracks by the way she looked. The question in her expression was demanding in its intensity. She reached out, grasped his leg around the ankle, and tugged on his jeans. Her eyes were wide and startled, her lips parted and inviting.

Something inside him shifted.

He gritted his teeth.

This woman was trouble.

Chapter Three

Lily didn't stay down. She was on her feet and moving as soon as he turned his back. An icy draft blew through the office as she lurched after the man ahead of her, but the sight that met her made her halt in the doorway, her breath trapped in her lungs as she stared down at the body sprawled on the floor. The sound of footsteps ringing on metal came from beyond. With one hand flat against the door, she pushed it wide open and peered in. Craning her neck, she saw that a window on the far side of the room was open and the man who had answered the door had gone out there, presumably onto the fire escape, after whoever had attacked this bloke on the floor.

What on earth had she walked into? Whatever she had been expecting from this date—and her mind had run the full gamut of possibilities, from delicious to disaster—she would never in a month of Sundays have expected to walk into a shootout.

The man on the floor groaned and moved his head slightly. He needed attention. Instinct kicked in. Her old nursing background took over. Darting to his side, she knelt down and took his pulse.

The injured man stirred, his eyes flickering open. "Lily, that's who is knocking at the door." He spoke vaguely, mumbling, his eyes not quite focused on her. "How could I have forgotten? Jesus, what a mess."

She stared down at him as everything fell into place. The man at the door wasn't Adrian. *This* was.

"She was due to arrive. Why didn't I remember?"

I know this man, I know him intimately.

His hand went to his head, and he pushed back his dark blonde hair. When he did, she saw a nasty red mark on his forehead. He tried to sit up, but she put her hand against his chest and steadied him. "Please try to stay still, you've got a head injury."

He groaned.

She'd never once needed her nursing skills outside of a job in her whole three years of training, but now that she'd stepped away from nursing it looked as if she was going to need it after all. She lifted his eyelids, examined his pupils, they looked normal. His eyes were hazel, she noticed. She loosened his tie, undid his collar, and held up her hand. "How many fingers do you see?"

"Three."

She moved her hand. "Now?"

"Two."

"What month is it?"

"January, it's the twenty-eighth."

"Good. Can you tell me where the pain is?"

"My head. Think I hit it on the desk. I ducked." He waved his hand in the direction of the window. "I was looking for my diary on the desk, then I dropped it on the floor. Heard the window breaking; saw someone out there."

"Do you have pain anywhere else?"

"Yes. Leg. Knee." His eyes flickered closed again.

She examined his limbs. He winced when she moved her hands around his right knee.

"It's a dodgy ligament, old injury, but I think I put it out when I dropped." The colour was draining from his face.

She stroked his cheek, gently reassuring him. "You're going to be okay, but that knock on the head is worrying me. I'll call an ambulance and get you checked out."

"No, you won't."

Lily's head snapped up. It was the other man, the man that she had been flirting with at the door — the man she'd been French kissing. The man who was obviously not Adrian, now. He'd climbed back in through the window and was approaching with determination, his expression overcast. She glared at the gun in his hand. "Please tell me you're with the police."

He nodded, then dropped to the floor on the other side of Adrian and put one large hand on the injured man's jaw, shifting it from side to side as he looked him over. "Come on, we have to get you out of here."

"Be careful with him," Lily exclaimed, shocked at his brusqueness. "He has a head injury, a knee injury, and he's at risk of concussion." She went to snatch his hand away from the injured man, but the other man locked his fingers around her wrist. His grip turned rigid. The stern, controlling look in his eyes silently informed her that she could only move if he allowed her to.

"This man needs to be checked at a hospital," she repeated, stubbornly, attempting again to jerk her arm from his grasp.

The dark-haired man held her tightly for a moment longer, to make his point, before letting her go. "He needs to be taken to a safe house is what he needs." His tone was stern, and he shook his head as if annoyed. "This man is a key witness in a criminal investigation. The longer he is in London, the more likely it is that someone will take another shot. I can't let that happen." He looked frustrated.

Lily was getting pretty frustrated herself. She couldn't follow what he was saying, and she didn't like his attitude. "Look, I know what I'm talking about. I used to be a nurse and I'm concerned about his head injury."

The dark-haired man ignored her and spoke to Adrian instead. "Are you convinced now?"

He'd got Adrian's attention. "Yes. I'm convinced, whatever you say, I'll do it." He let out a deep sigh.

"I thought so." The policeman shifted, drawing Adrian to his feet with one arm locked around his waist and back. Again he looked at Lily. "You get on the other side."

"I'll help you if you promise me you are taking him to the hospital."

He glared at her. "This man is in danger. The longer we hang around the more likely it is that someone will take another shot at him. Do you want that to happen?" His eyes were narrowed as he assessed her, looking her over as if he was suspicious of her.

"No, of course not, but..."

"Good, now can you help me out here?"

"Of course." The true nature of the situation was beginning to sink in. Her mouth was dry, shock making her shaky. "Anything I can do to help."

"I'm okay," Adrian said rising to his feet with their assistance. He winced when he tried to put weight on his right leg. "I'll just have to limp."

"Lean on us," the policeman instructed.

The policeman had a Welsh accent, Lily realised. Something about his voice had struck her, and that was it. Between them, they got Adrian to the elevator. When a couple of other people appeared in the corridor, the policeman warned them off, shouting at them to go back into their offices while he held out his ID in explanation.

Once they were inside the elevator, Adrian staggered into the corner and propped himself up. Lily checked his pupils again. "If you feel any nausea or dizziness, I want you to tell me immediately."

Adrian nodded, and then rested his head back against the wall and looked at her with curiosity. Heat rose in her face. He'd figured it out; he knew she was his date. She glanced away, confusion making her feel twitchy.

The policeman had reached into his pocket and pulled out a phone. Flicking it open, he called out. When she went to speak to him, he shook his head. "We've had an attempt. Our witness is injured, not fatal." There was bitter edge to his tone. "Yes, already, apparently good news travels fast."

Not fatal? Lily swallowed. The way he was talking, it was so...cold, and removed. The other bloke, Adrian, didn't seem surprised. He was staring ahead, his eyes thoughtful and his mouth tense.

"I need you to bring the vehicle right up against the front door, then get out and give the witness cover. The shooter may still be around."

He pushed the phone into his pocket and pulled out the gun, training it on the door just as they reached the ground floor.

His words echoed through Lily's mind. *He may still be around. The shooter.* A shudder went through her.

The other man, the policeman—as she now realised—fixed her with a demanding stare. "Ready?"

She nodded, and then wedged her shoulder firmly against the man she was holding up, securing his arm around her shoulders. Seconds later they were through the lobby, and out the door. A large four wheel drive vehicle was screeching to a halt on the pavement.

This can't be happening to me.

"Get out of the car," the policeman shouted to the driver. "Leave the key in the ignition and give me cover while I get the witness in." He snatched at the rear door, opening it for Adrian.

Lily caught a muffled query from the interior, and a moment later the driver emerged.

"I'm taking him out of the city. Tell the chief I have a good reason for what I am doing and I'll be in touch," shouted the policeman. Then he nodded at her and between them they got Adrian into the seat.

"You next. Get in." He had his hand on her shoulder.

"Excuse me?"

He glanced quickly around them as he responded. "You're coming with us to a safe house. It's for your own safety."

She shrugged him off. "No way. This has nothing to do with me."

"Sorry, sweetheart, but the moment you saw that man in the corridor it had everything to do with you. You are in danger and you are under my protection. Now get in."

Lily tried to walk away, but he grabbed her and jammed her up against the side of the car, using the full weight of his body to pin her there. From the base of her skull to the back of her knees she felt the cold, hard surface of the vehicle. Against her front, from breast to knee, his body crushed hers—warm, muscular, and overwhelmingly male.

His face was millimetres from hers, and he spoke between gritted teeth. "Get in the car."

She shook her head emphatically. "I've helped you with Adrian, now let me go."

"No." He had locked her in place, his hands either side of her on the car roof.

The man was a brute. She tried to wriggle free, unsuccessfully. Trapped there, she glared up at him. "This is intimidation."

"For Christ's sake!" There was outrage in his eyes, and as he grew frustrated with her his Welsh accent became even more apparent. "I'm not trying to intimidate you, I'm shielding you."

When she could finally drag her gaze away from his, she darted a glance around the busy street. She saw the lights flashing on the nearby pedestrian crossing, the people racing by on the pavement, people who didn't stop but were glancing their way, rubber-necking the scene. Was he out there, the man who had tried to shoot Adrian?

The other bloke, the driver, was flanking the far side of the vehicle, covering the door as if he expected someone to come after Adrian from that side. This couldn't be happening.

"But this has nothing to do with me," she repeated, her belief in that fact fast faltering. "I can't just leave. I have things to do."

"You're not safe here." The policeman grasped her chin with one hand, forcing her attention his way. He continued to talk in a low voice and it was heavy with warning. "Adrian is a witness in a gangland drugs running case. There's a hired killer with a gun out there, and it's my job is to protect him. Unfortunately the bloke clocked you in the corridor. I can't afford to leave you here because you're in danger as well."

He paused.

Lily swallowed. The nature of her involvement was fast becoming clear. That man, the one with the hard look, he was a killer. She really had walked into a crime scene. It made her want to get away from there as quickly as possible.

"Now we're getting somewhere," the policeman said, almost to himself, as he watched her reaction to his comments.

That riled her. She didn't want to conform to his orders. Besides, going with them would surely deepen her involvement. She tossed her hair back, glaring at him, unwilling to accept his authority over her. The action only seemed to heighten the full body contact between them. His body was all muscle, power and hard planes. A breathless exclamation escaped her in response to the sheer physical pressure he exerted over her.

For a moment, the world around them sped away. His eyelids lowered as her lips parted, his attention on her mouth. His was tight with tension, hard and unforgiving

38

and incredibly sexy. Minutes before, she had kissed that mouth. Now, danger was all around.

"Okay," she whispered, her voice choked.

He drew back from her, minimally, looked her over as if she were a nuisance, and then pushed her inside the car.

Her head was spinning, but when she got into the back seat instinct took over. Adrian was wedged awkwardly, and she slid in next to him and encouraged him to spread out and rest. Inside five seconds the policeman was in the driver's seat, door slammed behind him, foot to the floor. The vehicle screeched away from the pavement, and Lily reached for her seatbelt, wishing that her hands would stop shaking as she pushed it into place.

Adrian slumped against her, and she eased him into a more comfortable position so that his injured leg was up, the other foot wedged out of the way in the foot well. There didn't seem to be any alternative other than to have his head in her lap, but at least that meant she could keep a close eye on him.

"Just rest." She smoothed his hair back from his forehead, checking his pupils when the streetlights fell over him. He looked sharp and focused, but she had to be sure. She took off his loosened tie, folding it away.

"I'll need to check you every so often," she added. "I'll watch over you." Knowledge from her rather unsuccessful nursing career had kicked in, surprising her. Pleasing her, too. She didn't often get a chance to use it now.

"You're Lily, aren't you?"

She nodded. In the gloom, she could see that he was looking up at her, curiosity and acknowledgement in his eyes. Their intimate online connection set off a tide of mixed emotions, and she had to bite her lip to level herself. She was already upset and aggrieved about the situation she'd found herself in here. The reminder of why she was here in the first place only served to add to the confusion. When the street light reached him again, she saw that there was intimacy in his gaze.

"All this time I wondered what your voice would sound like." He gave a husky laugh and Lily's attention caught.

"Softer than I imagined," he added, very quietly, as if her ears alone. There was a seductive edge to that comment. It made her think of sex and of all the fantasies they had shared, her body heating instantly. "And so are you... You're beautiful, Lily. I'm so sorry you got dragged into this."

The car sped through the city, and the lights moved in strange patterns over the back seat, making the conversation seem even more surreal. "It's not your fault," she whispered, wanting to reassure him, this man who had given her so much pleasure over these last few weeks.

"Oh yes it is." He sighed heavily.

The scent of his cologne made her think of woodland space, not cars and the city and guns. Had he worn that cologne for their date, or did he wear it every day? She liked it, either way. In the passing lights she could see he grimaced in pain, his hand reaching for the knee that was up on the seat. She'd be a whole lot happier if he was checked out at a hospital. "Hey, try not to move around."

He nodded.

She put her hand to his forehead again, gently pushing back his hair so that she could check his head wound. One corner of his mouth lifted as he looked up at her. Her skin prickled with awareness as she thought about the things they had confessed to each other, and what she had hoped for from this date, her chest growing tight with emotion.

His hand closed over hers where it rested on his head, and he squeezed her gently. "It'll be okay, Lily, don't worry. Seth will make sure you're safe."

Seth. The policeman's name was Seth.

She nodded. When he closed his eyes, she turned away and looked out at the passing London streets. Where was the police officer taking them? What the hell had she walked into back there? She still didn't quite understand. It had all happened so fast. Then the questions melted away as she remembered the feeling she'd had when the driver, Seth, had answered the door. How it had felt when she had reached out and kissed him, thinking that he was all her dreams come true.

When she glanced in his direction, he was looking her way in the rear view mirror. Was he listening to what was said? Curiosity was there in his expression. She wasn't surprised. It wouldn't take a genius to work out that she was supposed to be meeting with Adrian. Instead, she'd thrown herself at him. The way she had come onto him in the corridor hung between them like static in the atmosphere — an unanswered question, a broken encounter. She looked away, and then back, studying him as he watched the road.

The oncoming lights highlighted his strong bone structure. Her hand itched to touch him again, her thoughts instantly running through what had happened between them in the corridor outside Adrian's office. He had short black hair, rugged features, and his dark brow shadowed intense blue eyes. Did he have to be so gorgeous? She'd been so ready to meet Adrian, and Adrian was attractive, too. Why was her life suddenly so complicated? She watched him until she saw his eyes flicker and once again he caught her attention in the rear view mirror. The tension heightened. Apparently he had eyes in the back of his head, because he seemed to know every time she looked his way.

Meanwhile, the man in her lap nestled down, an approving sigh escaping him as he settled in against her for the journey. She looked down at him, matching his warm smile with those words that echoed around her mind. This man knew so much about her.

With one hand, he stroked her arm, affectionately. His actions told her exactly how intimate her online relationship with him had been and she pressed her lips together, trying to steady her confused emotions after all that had happened.

Just then she caught sight of a road sign. They were headed west. Where? He'd mentioned a safe house. Wherever the hell they were going, it looked as if she was stuck with the pair of them—one bloke who she'd revealed all her intimate sexual fantasies to online, and another who she'd come on to before she even knew who he was.

Great, just great.

Her cheeks heated and she turned away, focusing on the flickering lights outside the window as the car sped on, headed out of the city.

Chapter Four

When Seth saw the big old house up ahead on the hillside, he slowed the car to a crawl, flicking his headlights down from full beam to sidelights. He didn't want to attract the attention of the neighbours. The nearest house was a good half a mile away, but on a clear night the lights could be spotted across the valley floor.

The lane that led up to the place where he had grown up was bumpy and Adrian woke up as they approached. "Where are we?" he asked as he sat up. "This doesn't look like 'an average Midlands housing estate' to me."

Seth noticed there was no lack of sharpness to Adrian's thinking. He'd remembered where they were supposed to be going. It was a safe bet that possible head injury could be ruled out.

"Wales," the woman responded, with a terse edge to her voice, "North Wales."

She hadn't rested for a moment. Watchful and alert, she'd pouted thoughtfully — and provocatively — all the way from London. Seth had felt her attention on him over the course of the journey, attention that was mutual. What was her role in this? She could be one of Carlisle's people. That was part of the reason he'd kept her close. He didn't want to think that, but he had to, because that was his job. Whatever their connection was, he wanted her under his watch so that he could monitor her.

"Wales?" Adrian repeated, and moved around in the back seat as he peered out of the window.

"Change of location," Seth said.

Adrian didn't respond.

Seth was relieved. He didn't want to explain why he had changed the plan. The less the witnesses knew, the safer they would be. The less anyone knew, in fact. Out there on that fire escape outside of Adrian's office, he'd caught sight of the assailant, and he'd recognised him. It was Emery Lavonne, a fellow officer in the force. That distinctive blond hair of his gave it away. Seth had just about kept a lid on his anger, but it had enraged him. He'd heard of good policeman being bought out, but he didn't understand that. Never would. Whatever, he needed time to think and he couldn't risk taking the primary witness to the designated safe house when Lavonne might already have got his hands on that address.

Instead he had brought them to *Hafod Y Coed,* a country hotel nestled in a wood in North Wales, the place where he had grown up.

Adrian attempted to read the sign as they passed, stumbling with the Welsh word structure. "What does it mean?"

"Summer woods," Seth responded. "It's a small private hotel, out of the way, and it's currently closed up for the winter season. We'll be using it as our safe house." Out of the way, that's why he'd opted for it. They didn't usually take witnesses into Wales, and it had seemed safer than booking into a regular hotel where the staff would be curious about who they were.

He pulled the Land Rover up in front of the building and wondered what his parents would say if they were in residence and he turned up with two strangers in tow, two people who were under his witness protection. Thankfully his parents were in Spain for their winter break. He switched off the ignition, then reached for the keys at his belt and sought out the one he hadn't yet used, the key his mother had given him.

"You never know when you might need to pop home," she'd said. They knew what sort of work he did. Maybe they thought someone would be on his back, one day, and he'd need to hide. "Keep it," she insisted, when he tried to tell her it wasn't necessary. "The alarm code is always the same, your birth date."

He'd never had to use it before. She'd always been at the door to greet him when he arrived on a visit.

Two minutes later he had the alarm switched off, and both his witnesses together with all the supplies from the car were in the hall. He walked to the system's control panel box and flicked on all the alarms and the heating. If he housed them in the rooms on this floor and at the back of the house, there would be less chance of the lights being seen by their distant neighbours.

When he turned back he saw that Adrian had sat down in the tall leather porter's chair—a much loved piece that his mother had found at a furniture auction—that stood in the reception area. The woman was peering up at the framed accommodation certificates on the wall and the brass plate that listed his parent's names as the license holders of the premises. When Adrian pulled up his trouser leg and groaned, the woman dropped to her knees beside him. "Oh my god, your leg is badly swollen."

"It's an old injury, a cartilage problem, but I think I've given it a jolt it as I went down."

Seth watched her tending Adrian. Once again he wondered what the hell the story was with these two. He'd been trying to figure it out all the way from London — that, and what the hell a cop was doing moonlighting for a lowlife like Carlisle.

"Do you have a first aid kit, with bandages?" The woman looked at Seth as she eased Adrian's shoe off. "This needs to be strapped for support."

Seth was already on it. He headed for the kitchen and was back a moment later, first aid case in hand. Setting the case down on the floor beside the porter's chair, he nodded at the woman. "You should find everything you need in there. I'll secure the place while you do so."

She was about to speak — and she looked pretty snippy — but he turned away before she had the chance to get started. Securing the place was his first priority. He checked the ground floor rooms, drawing closed the heavy curtains after he'd made sure the windows were locked. He lit the gas flamed log-fire in the residents' lounge and then headed into his stepfather's office, where he disconnected the phone and locked it in a drawer, pocketing the key.

Jogging up the stairs, he thought back over what action he'd taken, as he went — as he had done several times on the journey from London. He'd had to act on instinct back there, because the normal avenues were no longer an option. Even though it had been the best thing to do, he had to be sure. He always played by the rules, but when it had come to the crunch he had to step outside the boundaries. He'd taken the option he'd been trained to do: always protect the witness. Their chief, Stephen Ward, had always been adamant about that. But Seth had to take action fast, and those actions were all beyond his remit.

He checked the rooms on the first floor, assessing the security. The rooms were all dark and quiet. Taking them to the original safe house had no longer been an option. Lavonne would have access to the address. They could have gone to a hotel, but that involved other members of the public. That would have put more innocent people in danger, and every single person who knew where they were opened up a potential risks. He paused and scanned the road from a window, he saw no lights. Lavonne wouldn't find them here. He squinted into the darkness. They had not been tailed, and he had no intention of using a phone that could be tracked by sat. His job –and his nature — didn't let him rest easy though, not yet.

On the top floor of the building his parents had their private living accommodation. He jogged up the next set of stairs, locked the door to that part of the building, and added the key to his fob. He'd done the best thing under the circumstances. Brooding on it, he wrapped his hand around the back of his neck. Pieces of a jigsaw were falling into place. His department had lost the last two high profile witnesses under protection. It had been devastating to their team, and now Seth knew why it had happened. Lavonne was a turncoat in their midst. It made Seth's gut knot with anger.

He could try to get word to his boss, when the time was right. He knew what Stephen would say, he would tell him that his priority was his witness, and the woman who could finger Lavonne. That's why he had fast-tracked to a new plan. There was no way that snake Lavonne was taking these two out, no way. And if he knew she could ID him, he'd want the woman as much as he'd want Adrian Walsh, because she could identify him. *And me. He'll have to take me out, or be exposed.*

Each and every protection duty was life and death to Seth Jones, but this one had now become a challenge and a duty above and beyond everything that had gone before. He put his hand against the locked door to the private apartment at the top of the house. This was home, this was off the radar, and this location was entirely unknown to Lavonne. If they kept their heads down, they were safe. He'd done the right thing.

Patting the door, he smiled to himself. *Thanks Mum*, he thought, before he headed back downstairs.

By the time he got back down to the ground floor Lily had bandaged Adrian's leg and had his foot raised up on a footstool. She was kneeling beside the chair and they were deep in conversation. Seth slowed down as he approached and tried to catch what was being said.

"No, I arrived there maybe a minute or so early. When I got to your office there was a bloke hanging around in the corridor. He gave me a really filthy look, but then he went out of the window and I assumed he was a maintenance man. Obviously not." She looked at Adrian, and he shook his head, his expression overcast.

Seth noticed then how they were with each other, conversing like old pals. It was odd because there was a suggestion of closeness, and yet they can't have met before because Lily had thought he himself was Adrian. Intriguing.

"I knocked..." She paused and glanced towards the staircase. When she saw he had returned, her cheeks flushed and her eyelids lowered. "And your friend answered the door." She nodded her head in Seth's direction. "Then I heard gunshots and I was pulled inside the office."

Seth stifled a smile. She'd rather conveniently abbreviated her story to cover her error. He watched her, but she didn't look back at him.

Adrian reached out and rested his hand on her arm, squeezing it gently. "It's my fault you're here. I am so sorry you've got mixed up in this."

"I've put the fire on in the main sitting-room," Seth interrupted. "If you'd like to convene in there, we'll run through some ground rules."

The woman, Lily, was on her feet in a flash, pulling her short coat around her as if readying to leave. "I don't want to convene anywhere." She spoke tersely, but that embarrassed flush was still on her cheekbones. "How long are you going to keep me here?"

"At the outside, until Adrian gives evidence at trial."

"When is that?"

"Two weeks."

Her eyes rounded. "I can't stay here for two weeks!"

Seth noticed how sexy she looked when she was outraged. Would she look that way if he reminded her about their first encounter? The idea of it turned him on. He had to stifle a smile in order to concentrate on getting her on board, which was the number one priority right now. Anything else could wait a while. "Unfortunately you've seen too much. None of us want to be here, but there's an issue of safety and justice involved. Adrian is giving evidence at a trial. He's in danger, and now you are too, because of what you've seen."

"I could go home. Nobody knows me or where I live."

Seth looked at her. He hated to see anyone this uncomfortable with the set up, but there wasn't a choice. Lavonne's status was his burden. Trying a different tactic, he shrugged. "Adrian here is a friend of yours, yes?"

Maybe that wasn't a good move. Heat flared in her face and she shifted uncomfortably. He had to get to the bottom of this. It set a thread of doubt loose. What was it with these two? Was it anything to do with Carlisle? He had to know, and soon.

"Yes, we are friends."

That was carefully worded. "Consider how he feels. He doesn't want to be here either, this is a stressful time. Your support would be helpful."

She glanced at Adrian and quieted. Adrian lifted his hands in a silent apology.

"Adrian is my charge," Seth continued, "but you have inadvertently become a secondary witness and you can ID the man who made an attempt on Adrian's life." He looked at her to gauge her understanding. She seemed to be taking it in. "My duty is to protect you both until the danger has passed." He gestured towards the sitting room door and gave her an encouraging smile "If you'd like to come this way, we can have a chat and get settled in."

She didn't return his smile. Instead, she shook her head dismissively. "Do I have my own room here?"

He'd made a slight inroad with her, but she was still reluctant. "You do, but before I show you to your room, I need to request you hand over your mobile phones to me. Both of you."

Her eyebrows drew together and her lips tightened.

This was the worst part—people and their mobile phones were inseparable. It was their last little bit of independence and it was always hard for them. "It's for your safety. The house phone is also disconnected."

Adrian rummaged in his trouser pocket. A moment later he handed his phone over. Seth took it and put it on the sideboard that stood against one wall in the hallway. The guest ledger was there, and he closed it as he put the phone down. He put out his hand to the woman. She had a small bag over her shoulder that rested on the opposite hip. It was large enough for a phone and a wallet, maybe some make up. She glared at him for the longest moment, then reluctantly opened the bag and handed her phone over. "This is ridiculous," she muttered.

"Thank you. I assure you that it's standard procedure and it's done with your safety in mind. Now, I can show you your room, or if you'd like to take a seat in the sitting-room, I'll organise some tea and sandwiches. Your rooms will be on this floor, and the radiators will have them warned up in just a few minutes. Meanwhile, let's relax in front of the fire." He looked back at the woman. She was his main problem.

She pulled her coat closed around her. "I'm tired. I'd like to go to my room now."

Seth studied her. She didn't look tired at all. In fact she looked wired. Was this because she'd embarrassed herself, or was there another reason? There was only one way to find out—give her a little bit of leeway and she might relax enough to talk about it. He nodded at her.

Gesturing at the nearby doorway for room number three, he selected the room that was almost opposite the sitting-room. He could keep an eye on her from there, just in case she had any dubious plans of her own. "Oh," he said, when she began to move in the direction of the doorway, "please don't attempt to open the windows. The alarm is set to go off if anyone enters...or leaves."

When she reached for the door handle, she flashed him an annoyed look.

Seth turned away. "Let's get you into the sitting room," he said as he put his arm around Adrian's shoulders and lifted him bodily from the chair. "I think there are a couple of walking sticks in the office, I'll fetch you one later. Right now I want to get you comfortable."

"Cheers mate," Adrian said, and hopped alongside him.

As they passed room number three, the door closed.

While Seth got Adrian propped up on a sofa with a bunch of cushions holding his leg up, it occurred to him that the knee injury would keep this one exactly where he wanted him. Lily, the woman was not going to be so easily grounded. He flicked the TV on and then nodded at Adrian. He looked a bit washed out but not too much worse for wear. There was a bit of discoloration where he had knocked his forehead, but it could have been way, way worse. "I bet you could use a cup of tea?"

Adrian smiled. "That would be great, thanks."

As Seth wended his way to the kitchen, he made a mental list of what had to be done. First up he had to find out the nature of the relationship between these two. Secondly, he had to get the woman on board. Then he had to figure a way to let his boss know about Lavonne, without revealing their new location. He couldn't risk it leaking in the office. He didn't know Emery Lavonne well enough to be sure of his next move, but Seth could guess. If Emery knew that he'd been spotted, he'd been even more determined to do the job and cover his tracks. That was why he had to let his chief know they had a mole in their midst, but he had to do it carefully.

* * * *

"Tea up."

Adrian groaned as he woke up. He'd dozed off in the armchair and now Seth was holding out a mug of tea to him.

"Thanks."

"How are you feeling?"

"Fine. Just tired." It was a lie. He hurt like hell. His head throbbed and his knee had seized up. Every slight move was painful.

"I'll fetch you that walking stick, then I'll get you some painkillers and make us some food."

"Got any whisky? Or brandy?" He seemed to ache everywhere and his knee was shot to hell, pain burning up the length of his thigh.

Seth, the witness protection officer, nodded at the back of the room. "We do indeed have access to a small bar here."

Adrian glanced over the back of the sofa. In the far corner of the room he saw a hand built oak bar. There were shelves on the wall filled with bottles, a rack of wine bottles and a couple of kegs of beer. Adrian beamed. "Ace. You didn't mention that when you were trying to talk me into this. That would have made your job a whole lot easier."

Seth gave a dry laugh. "It's a small residential hotel. The place is shut up for the winter, but it's secluded. That comes with pros and cons."

Adrian put his hand up. "The bar is a pro. Don't bother me with the cons right now. It's been a long day."

Seth nodded, and drank his tea. After a moment he nodded his head at the door to the hallway. "What's the situation with you and the woman?"

Adrian shook his head. "Shit, I feel so bad about Lily. I'd completely forgotten she was due to arrive."

"Blind date?"

Adrian frowned. How did he know that? For all he knew they'd already discussed it. He'd been fading in and out all evening. "Kind of. Well...put it this way, we hadn't met before this evening." He scrubbed his hand through his hair, mentally kicking himself that he'd forgotten.

Seth nodded. "Is she involved in any way with Carlisle? Is that how you met?"

Adrian half sat, amazed that the officer had even thought that. "God no, not at all. We've known each other for longer than that."

"I didn't think there was a connection," Seth commented, "but I need to check everything, you know?"

"Yes, I see." He frowned, working back in his mind. "There's no connection. Lily and I met on the net, in an online chat room, way back, before Carlisle employed me. We'd arranged to meet properly tonight, that's all." Adrian sighed and sank back into the cushions. He was gutted that *Laidbacklady* been dragged into this because of him, and he wished he could turn back the clock. "Was she really in danger, I mean, did you really have to bring her here with us?"

Seth took another deep swig of his tea—eyes fixed on the flickering flames of the faux log fire—before answering.

"I'm afraid so. She clocked the bloke who was sent in for you, I couldn't risk leaving her in London."

Adrian waited for more information, but apparently the man said as little as possible. Adrian thought about what little he had said, and a tsunami of guilt washed over him. "Christ. What a mess."

"Not really. All we have to do is lay low until the court case. If your friend tows the line, she's safe."

Adrian nodded, relieved.

"She's a very attractive woman," Seth commented.

Adrian nodded. "You can say that again." Would she hate him for this? She had every right to do so. "I should go talk to her, apologise."

"You need to rest, and she needs time to get used to this. She's upset. You've had a bit longer to come to terms with it."

"That's true." He looked at the door, concerned about her and how she must be feeling right now.

"I'll check on her, okay?" Seth got to his feet. "I'll get you some food first."

"Brandy," Adrian bartered.

"Food, then brandy. You know it makes sense."

"You drive a hard bargain." Adrian forced a smile he didn't really have the energy for, and gave Seth a thumbs-up.

When Seth had gone, he let out a deep sigh and settled back on the sofa. If only he hadn't taken the Carlisle contract. None of this would be happening. He might have been having dinner with Lily instead, getting to know her properly. Instead she was in her room hating him for what he'd dragged her into. Life played some weird tricks on a man. Reaching back, he punched the cushion behind his head, pushing it more forcefully into the crook of his neck.

Then again, if I hadn't been on edge about Carlisle, I might never have asked her out and I might never have looked into those sexy eyes. His head throbbed, and he mumbled half-heartedly, cursing as he closed his eyes, giving in to the urge to doze.

Chapter Five

Lily couldn't rest, no matter how hard she tried. Instead, she paced up and down the narrow passage between the twin beds in her designated room, trying to come to terms with her situation. It wasn't easy. She was in some sort of protective custody, in the depths of the Welsh countryside. The building they were in was an old manor house, done out like some sort of hotel. Not what she was expecting, but then she wasn't sure what to expect. Being thrust into witness protection was way beyond her personal experience.

The room reminded her of an old youth hostel she'd stayed at years ago, except that place was sparsely furnished with bunk beds and this was comfortably furnished and kind of plush, if a bit tweedy and old-fashioned. It made her think of Fawlty Towers, and she had a slightly crazed laugh at the idea of it, flopping on to the nearest bed.

There was a portable TV on a bedside cabinet and she turned it on, watching the news and yet feeling as if it were about a different planet to the one she currently inhabited. After a while she got up again, too restless to concentrate, and stepped into the en suite bathroom. She peered at herself in the mirror, for the third time that evening. She didn't look too bad, considering. Her mascara was smudged and her eyes were a bit wild, otherwise she looked as if she had just had a night out on the town. If only. Sighing, she tugged the bathroom light cord, and went back into the bedroom that she had been designated. True to her captor's word, the room had warmed up quickly, despite the high ceilings and the fact the place had obviously been empty a while. She glanced around.

"How long am I going to be stuck here?" She stood with her back against the old-fashioned Victorian radiator warming her hands and legs and stared around the strange bedroom while she tried to make sense of everything that happened over the course of the evening. The witness protection officer, Seth, had taken charge as if it was his god given right. He'd been so high-handed and arrogant that her back was well and truly up. She balked at following his instructions, and she expected at least a modicum of respect—especially if Adrian and she were such highly valued members of the public that they needed his protection. He riled her. Then there was the fact she'd accidentally gotten intimate with him, which apparently had given him an excuse to act as if he owned her. Was he that way with everyone?

The question made her remember each and every detail of what had happened between them, and her response to the memory was physical as well as mental. Tossing her hair back, she pushed the memories away as best she could. One thing was for sure, she wanted her phone back.

She had to get in touch with her flatmate. Andrea would be worried sick. They worked together, and they had a business to run. Andrea knew she was out on a date but if she wasn't there in the morning Andrea would have to bring in a temp, and they couldn't afford that right now.

After a moment she gathered her resolve and listened at the door. Clicking it open, she found that the hallway was now in darkness. Across the corridor light poured out of an open doorway. She could hear the sound of the television and the two men exchanging comments. Somebody laughed, and for a moment she was tempted to join them. On principle, she denied herself that luxury.

It'd been hard, because her curiosity was raging—about both of them. Adrian, the man who she had been so intimate with online, and Seth the arrogant man who was now in charge. *Phone*, she reminded herself. As her eyes grew accustomed to the gloom she could see that the two phones were still sitting on the hall table, where he had left them.

Opening the door a little wider, she winced when it squeaked. Squeezing through the narrow gap, she took a deep breath and darted across the hallway. She had the phone in her hand when a tall shadow blocked the light from the sitting-room doorway.

"Don't even think about it." Seth was beside her inside four paces, his expression overcast and inscrutable. He removed the phone from her hand, flipped it over and showed her the back panel.

Lily's mouth tightened when she saw that he'd removed the SIM Card. She glared at him. He'd left the phones there as bait, the bastard. "I suppose you think that's funny."

A half-smile broke the stern look on his face, and that only served to emphasise his dominant hold over her. Lily didn't want to hear whatever smart remark was about to come out of his mouth. Turning on her heel she went back to her room, but when she went to close the door she found it blocked by the weight of his body. Her pulse tripped and then raced on.

Seth stepped inside, closing the door behind him. It was then that she was reminded of exactly how large he was. His physique was solid and strong. He'd abandoned his leather jacket and the shirt he wore was closely fitted, revealing the breadth of his shoulders and the narrowness of his waist and hips.

"What do you want?" She issued the question sternly and then folded her arms across the chest, every pulse point in her body aware of his presence. The way he was looking at her—with a slow and obvious up-and-down perusal of her body—left her in no doubt of what he wanted. *Great, I kissed the man, and now he thinks he has rights.*

"We need to talk." He was so still, so contained, and yet everything about him suggested action. "I need your compliance. I want you to do as I say while you are under my protection." He paused. "But you don't like following instructions, do you?"

Her spine straightened. She glanced away, blocking out the thoughts that surfaced. He'd hit a nerve there, but she wasn't about to let him know that. "I don't like being pulled out my life over something that has nothing to do with me."

He looked at her, steadily. "I understand that. Believe me, if you were aware of all the circumstances you'd be glad you are in witness protection." He paused again, and one corner of his mouth lifted. "In fact, you might even play nicely."

"You reckon?" She threw him a sarcastic glance.

That only seemed to amuse him.

"Why don't you come across the hallway and be social?"

The smile that hovered around his mouth made her lips part as she thought about how that mouth felt under hers, and how brazenly she'd acted when she thought he was Adrian. She wasn't ready to go in there and 'be social', because there was no way she could sit with the two of them and chit-chat, not yet.

He took a step closer, and it was with such deliberate intent — his eyes never leaving hers — that her heart missed a beat. Frustrated, she lashed out. "Okay, you win. I can't make any calls. But my flatmate will report me missing if she doesn't hear from me, I know she will."

He frowned. "That may or may not be good news."

There was no way she was going to flatter him by asking what his cryptic comment meant. "Look, I need some time alone to get my head around all of this."

He stared at her for the longest moment, and then nodded. But he didn't make a move to leave. In fact he looked rooted to the spot.

"Keep an eye on Adrian," she said, hurriedly, feeling guilty about that, "concussion can come on several hours after the injury."

"Don't worry, I will. He's doing okay, he's just a bit shaken up and that's understandable." That did set her mind at rest, but he was still focused on her, seemingly unwilling to leave. "And you need to eat," he added. "I've made you a sandwich, I'll fetch it."

Why was it that everything he said annoyed her? "You're too kind."

"I'm trying. Believe me." A sardonic smile passed briefly over his face.

The way he smiled made Lily realise how rarely it happened, but when he did, it was thoroughly wicked. His eyes were dark with secret thoughts.

"I'm not your enemy here, Lily, please try to remember that."

His comment struck a chord, and the way he said her name—as soft as a caress—made her breath hitch. His glance was brooding, sexual. It was also intimate, and somehow intrusive. It made her feel frustrated with him, and yet it made her feel outrageously horny, too. She knew she should put her foot down, tell him to get out of the room, and yet the fact he was there at all secretly thrilled her. Wired to every sensation, to every atmospheric change in the room, her skin prickled.

"This would all be so much more pleasant if you chilled out." Eyebrows lifted, he went further. "We could act as if we were meeting for the first time, like we did earlier today."

The bastard, he had to bring that up—and there was a suggestive glint in his eye as he reminded her of it. She shook her head. "You've had your fun with the phone, leave me alone."

"You don't mean that." They were inches apart and he was studying her as if he was aware of how turned on she was by his presence.

"Don't I?" Her body was a mass of conflicting signals. Her blood raced and she was finding it difficult to control her breathing.

Moving quickly, he grasped her around her wrist with one determined hand and drew her arm away from her chest, taking away her shield. His hand felt warm and yet unyielding as he held her wrist, and her other arm automatically fell to her side.

"We have unfinished business, and you know it."

Unnerved, she tried to pull away, but when he held on to her and drew her closer still, she melted. "No. That was a mistake. I thought you were Adrian," she whispered. "That's why I kissed you."

That didn't faze him.

"I know. It was a blind date, but you liked what you saw, didn't you? You made your move, and you made it on me." He said it so suggestively, and for some reason his Welsh accent seemed to key into a deep part of her.

"You're an arrogant prick." Even so, the memory of what she'd said and done raced through her mind over again, hammering the point home. Her face was on fire.

"Thing is," he said, running one finger down her top and around the outside of her breast, making her head spin, "I enjoyed it, and I think you did too."

There was no answer to that. She couldn't deny it, not after what had happened, and now his thumb rested over her knotted nipple, applying just enough pressure through her top and bra to make her crazy. She'd well and truly dropped herself in it with this man, and by the looks of it he was going to torture her for his own amusement.

When she didn't respond, he continued. "Unfortunately I was distracted, and that wasn't very gentlemanly of me, not while you were being so generous with your affections." He lifted her chin with one sure finger. "I feel we should try again, and this time I'll give you my full and undivided attention."

Before she had a chance to deny him or respond, he kissed her full on the mouth. Lily could do nothing to stop it. Her hands instinctively went to his chest, with the intention of pushing him away. When she tried to do so she couldn't seem to apply any pressure. His body was hard and powerful, and hers gravitated closer as her lips parted. His mouth claimed hers, thoroughly, his tongue teasing hers. His hands moved over her bottom, squeezing it through her skirt, holding her against his hard hips so she could feel his erection growing.

I can't do this. Breathlessly, she broke free, and yet her hands still stroked across his chests and shoulders, learning him, her body pivoting on one heel and her hips locked against his. "You're just trying to embarrass me."

"No, not at all. I'm trying to make you relax."

"Yeah, right." Looking into his eyes she saw that he really meant it. Could it be true? Even if it was true, it didn't stop her being embarrassed. She shrugged his comment off. "Is this what you do to all of the witnesses under your so-called protection?"

He lifted her, bodily, and turned her around, pressing her up against the wall in a flash, his hands sliding her skirt up the sides of her hips. "No," he said, voice husky and intimate, "but you're the only one who has ever come on to me before we were even introduced." His eyes flickered. "That makes you pretty damn memorable. Besides, you gave me an invitation I don't intend to let you revoke."

Christ, he was so full-on, and her body burned in response to his hands on her. "What the hell are you doing?"

He ducked down and planted a hungry kiss on her throat. "Touching you…everywhere I think you need to be touched." His hand was under the front of her skirt and it closed over her knickers, cupping the mound of her pussy and making her gasp aloud. He lifted his head, and nodded. "Oh yes, you're hot. You did enjoy it, didn't you?"

"I thought you were Adrian," she shot at him, annoyed, and then moaned involuntarily when he squeezed her pussy. The action took her breath away.

"So you keep saying."

Her clit burned and pulsed inside the hard cup of his palm, and she shifted from one foot to the other.

He moved one leg against the outside of hers, caging her in. "But it's me now, touching you, and your underwear is damp in my hand…how…shocking." He tutted mockingly while he massaged her pussy, ignoring her feeble, half-hearted attempts to push him away.

"You bastard." Her arms felt weak, and her head tipped back against the surface of the wall for balance. Her eyes closed as pleasure filled her groin, her core clamping, aching to be filled by that hard cock he had pressed against her hip.

Then he pushed his hand inside her knickers and one finger sank into her damp groove, brushing over her swollen clit. Her pulse beat wildly in response.

"Tell me you want me to stop, and I will." He paused, loosening his hold, teasing one finger along the damp, sensitive lips of her sex.

"I…" Her head rolled from side to side.

He roved deeper and stroked her clit.

Once.

Aching need shot through her.

Her core spasmed and she squirmed, her hips rolling. "Don't stop," she begged, unable to help herself. "Please don't stop…"

With consummate skill he stroked his finger back and forth over her clit, teasing her orgasm to the surface. He held her gaze while he did so, watching her as she climaxed—as if every moment fascinated him. That alone would have pushed her to the edge, but his finger had already become her master. She was lost to the experience, and seeing his reaction only made her peak come all the faster. Her breath hitched in her chest and she moaned aloud. Latching her hands over his shoulders, she held on tight.

Release barrelled through her.

Her legs buckled and the inside of her thighs was slick wet.

Strong arms held her up.

It was through a haze of pleasure that she became aware of his mouth on her jaw. He kissed her softly, his breath warm on her alert skin. She jerked back, confused by him, and confused by what had happened. He lifted his head and smiled knowingly at her. A moment later he stepped away and walked to the door, leaving her slumped against the wall with her skirt hitched up around her hips, dazed and panting.

He's going to walk out, right now, she realised.

She glared at his back as she pulled her skirt back into place. "You've just gone and made it even harder for me to leave this room!"

He paused with his hand on the door handle and looked back at her. Humour filled his expression. "You can do it. I have faith in you." He looked her up and down. "Oh, I'll bring you that sandwich. You'll need sustenance."

I hate you, she thought, as she watched him leave, wishing that he was staying, instead.

Chapter Six

Dawn broke, the icy morning mist lingering around the red brick housing estate. Emery Lavonne pulled the collar on his jacket closer around his neck and watched the safe house through narrowed eyes, his cheeks grinding with annoyance, his huffed breath hanging in the atmosphere. It was a plain suburban detached house on a postage stamp of land, surrounded by identical houses. The only difference was this one was empty. It shouldn't be.

Lavonne had headed straight for the Midlands after he'd seen Seth Jones removing the witness. The fact that they hadn't turned up here was bad news. Why? Throughout the night he'd hidden in the bushes, having sought out a good viewing point, but now he emerged and glared at the place unchecked. Jones had obviously not followed the plan he had been given.

An attempt on the witness's life would have unsettled him. Would that have been enough to make him deviate from the plans that had been set in motion at headquarters, or had there been a last-minute change? Jones was seen as a stalwart of the department, he never usually broke any rules, but he'd also never lost a witness. He wouldn't want a black mark on his record now. Lavonne had been in the office earlier that day, when Seth Jones left for his one-on-one time with the witness. Either it was a last-minute change in safe house, or Jones had reacted to the attempt. Whichever it was, it was bad news. He didn't need complications. This had to be quick and clean. Plan A, take the witness down before he left London. Plan B, track Seth Jones and his witness, preferably getting to the safe house before they got there. He was going to have to figure out plan C, and fast.

Lavonne cursed Seth Jones. He had always got his back up and doubly so now he was the officer on the case. What he couldn't figure was why Jones had taken another person, a woman, with him. Was she Adrian Walsh's girlfriend? The paperwork hadn't indicated the witness had a wife or a partner, but Lavonne had seen Seth with a woman by the car. Walsh had been inside the vehicle. He couldn't see her face, but he'd watched from a side street as Jones took them both into safe custody, and he was annoyed that he'd missed a chance. It didn't matter. He'd simply take down his target at the new safe house, or wherever the fuck Seth had taken them.

He checked the time. It was close to seven, and he had to leave now in order to get back to London and the office. Casting one last glance over the safe house, he left. He'd parked his car five streets away, and he was jogging in that direction when his mobile phone bleeped. Flicking it open, he saw that it was Jason Keane, his contact for the hit. Grimacing, he considered not answering it. He wanted to get on the road, but this might be important. He didn't want the job to go to someone else because he'd ignored the call.

He answered. "Yes."

"Progress?"

"I'll be on the system today. I'll have the safe house address before the day is out."

Silence. "You told me you had it already."

"I want to be sure," Lavonne lied. He'd reached his parked car and climbed inside, more comfortable now he couldn't be overheard. "Leave it with me, you won't be disappointed."

"There is no room for disappointment." Keane paused. "Remember that."

Lavonne gritted his teeth for a moment before allowing himself to respond. "The sooner you hang up, the sooner I can do this."

"Sure, but I want to meet you."

Lavonne's hand tightened on the phone. He sensed Keane was enjoying this. Could he afford the risk of being seen with him? "Why? Is that necessary? It's all time-wasting."

"Mr Carlisle asked me to meet with you in person. He's happy with the arrangement and with the fee you named. I'll pay you fifty percent now, fifty percent when the job is done."

"Fair enough." The money was only a small part of it for Lavonne, but he wasn't about to admit that. He had his own reasons, and he had inside information. He'd offered to take out the key witness and Keane had taken the bait. He didn't mention that he'd already made an attempt. There was a chance it would be on the news, but there would be a cover up, given the witness status. He'd taken a chance, tried to hit the target before they left the city.

Slight error of judgement there, but there would be another time, and this time he wouldn't fail.

"Mr Carlisle likes to be kept informed, which means I have to touch base with you every few hours. Believe me, I'd rather do the job myself and not have to deal with you. You're a cop and I don't trust cops."

Lavonne resisted the urge to be sarcastic. Jason Keane was a drug dealer and a jumped up lackey, but he didn't want to antagonise him. "The target is already off the public radar. The important thing is I'll take care of it, and quickly."

"Good, because Mr Carlisle doesn't like his cell. It's not up to his usual standards."

"Trust me, I'm on it."

"You'd better be, because I'm on you, and you won't shake me free until we are done with this."

Mouth twitching with annoyance, Lavonne shut his phone and rammed his keys in the ignition.

* * * *

Seth's sarcastic "I have faith in you" remark did encourage Lily to venture out of her room, but not until the following morning. She'd spent most of the night alternately fuming, getting aroused, being embarrassed, and brooding on her situation, until eventually she passed out with exhaustion. Around eight she awoke. All was quiet in the building. By the time she had showered and dressed she'd been able to chuckle to herself, having finally seen the funny side of his teasing remark the night before.

Of course she could do it.

She'd been brave enough to meet up with her virtual lover, she'd flirted madly with a stranger who'd subsequently seduced her, and she'd even stuck her tongue out at him when he'd delivered her sandwich the night before. Going out there and facing the pair of them was simply the next step in a catalogue of mistakes and humiliations. Keeping her sense of humour was clearly paramount.

The fact that her curiosity was getting the better of her also proved to be good motivation. What were the two of them doing out there, she constantly wondered as she stared at the door. Late into the night she'd heard the TV, and later on some chatter and laughter. Had they been discussing her? Before she let herself ponder that one too much and lost her nerve as a result, she grabbed the door handle and left her room.

Further down the corridor was a door with a sign that read 'Residents' Lounge'. That's where Seth had emerged from the night before, when she'd tried to grab her phone. The door was open, and she headed over and ducked her head in. It was thankfully empty of attractive men this morning, so she made her way across the gloomy room and peeped through the curtains to have a good look around and get her bearings.

Large French windows overlooked a patio and frost-covered evergreen borders, and the view beyond was postcard-pretty with bare, frosted trees and distant hills dotted with sheep. The room itself was large and comfortable. There were several well-stuffed armchairs and a matching sofa. One wall was lined with books. There was also a TV, a rack of DVDs, and what looked like a well-stocked bar in one corner of the room.

Braving the corridor again, she noticed that the doors to room number one and two were both slightly ajar. The sound of a shower running emerged from at least one doorway. She headed in the opposite direction, towards the staircase. To the left of it she saw an open doorway that led into the kitchen.

Whoa, this place is a dream. Andrea would love it. It was just the sort of thing they wanted for their business, but they couldn't stretch to it as yet. She walked along the stainless steel cooker tops and work surfaces, running her fingers over them possessively. A massive great breakfast bar ran down the centre of the room, two stainless steel poles reaching from floor to ceiling at either end giving the place a high-tech, all-mod-cons feel that didn't quite fit with the rest of the house. Whoever did the cooing here liked their gadgets. As she passed, she loosely clasped the pole at one end, pivoting on one heel, imagining what Andrea would say if she could see this fabulous kitchen.

"Oh yes, you like that, don't you?"

Lily turned on her heel, her hand falling way from the pole.

Adrian was standing in the doorway, elbow up against the frame as he supported his weight on one leg, a walking stick in his other hand. His insinuating gaze was on her shimmying with the pole.

Her skin prickled anxiously and she quickly moved away from the metal pole when she realised what she'd done. Without thought, she had sashayed across the space by instinct, using the pole as her pivoting point.

It was there in his eyes; he remembered everything she'd said — that fantasy about being a pole dancer or a lap dancer for a private audience, one special man. Part of her wanted the floor to open up and swallow her. The other part of her responded to the intimate knowledge held in his gaze. Isn't that what she wanted, someone who would know her secret desires without her having to say them aloud? Yes, but she hadn't known then that it would work out like this, that she would be locked into a place and time with him that she couldn't just get up and walk away from. Flustered, she rebuked his comment. "You're embarrassing me."

He smiled, and there was gentleness and fondness there in his expression. "I know, and I'm sorry. I couldn't resist when I saw you there and remembered." He was a good man. More subtle than she'd thought he would be. He winked and the tension she felt dissipated a little. "I wouldn't have thought it possible to embarrass you, not when we were exchanging explicit messages in that chat room."

Somehow she felt rooted to the spot, trapped by the amused accusation in his expression. She wanted to be that brave woman who had chatted with him so explicitly, but right now it was hard to muster it up. "It was easier then and we talked about that, we both knew it wouldn't be as easy when we met."

There was a defensive tone to her voice that she resented. Glancing back over her shoulder as she walked over to the kettle, she saw that Seth was standing in the doorway, watching them. Could this get any more difficult? Above all she craved to be braver, but it seemed beyond her grasp because they were here and not in London, and Seth was part of the equation she hadn't bargained on. She took a deep breath in, focusing on the kettle. How long had he been there? How much had he heard? Steeling herself, she grabbed the kettle as she passed. "I guess—seeing as I am the woman in this set up—I should put the kettle on and make us some tea."

She delivered the statement with a note of sarcasm, eager to move the topic of conversation on. But even as she busied herself at the sink, filling the electric kettle, she felt their eyes on her and she remembered why she had wanted to be a private dancer for a man who wanted her.

It had been on the lead up to Christmas, and she and Andrea and a mixed group of friends had gone to a lap-dancing club in Soho, for a laugh. It had turned into something else for Lily as she watched the dancers shimmy and slide, and she felt the sensual power delivered in their actions. She wanted that, to exhibit her sensuality, to strut and tease and to have a man grow eager for her as she displayed herself. The fantasy had shocked her at first, still did if she was honest, but she hadn't been able to shrug it off. Inevitably, it had come out during her chats with Adrian.

She heard the clunk of Adrian's stick behind her. "Remember our agreement?"

She turned to look at him, ignoring the looming presence of Seth beyond him—trying also to ignore the fact Seth had brought her to orgasm so ruthlessly the night before.

Adrian's eyes were filled with concern, and there was reassurance there, too. "We agreed that if it didn't work out, it didn't work out. No big deal. I'm sorry you got dragged into this. This situation has taken away the element of choice we discussed, so everything that went before is null and void...unless you say different..."

Looking into his eyes, she saw his kindness. She also saw the blatantly flirtatious nature she knew from the chat rooms. Deeper still, raw desire. He wanted her. He'd met her for real and he still wanted her. *Unless you say different.*

It was a suggestion. He wanted her to say different; he wanted her to act on their connection. In the pit of her belly she acknowledged that, her core growing warm and supple with yearning. Staring at him, her mind flooded with the sexual scenarios she had envisaged on meeting him. *This man knows me. This man knows what I want.* She nodded, unable to express more right then, not with Seth listening.

"The last thing I want is for you to feel awkward around me. I'm sorry about teasing you. You just looked so good." He nodded at the pole, and then looked back at her.

She couldn't bring herself to reply, because he'd remembered what she had said. She'd never met a man who had remembered what she'd said about her desires, not before now. Seth was watching, too. Dense heat was gathering inside her, her pussy fluttering, an ache of need flaring at her core as words flashed through her mind, words she and Adrian had exchanged. Her libido had been well and truly triggered, and she was only pulled out of it when she felt cold water splashing over her hand. She groped for the tap. She hadn't even realised the kettle was full to overflowing.

Adrian reached across her, dropping his stick to the floor as he took charge and turned off the tap. "It's my fault that you're here," he said as he straightened up. "I'll never forgive myself for that. No more teasing. I promise."

She shrugged. It wasn't really his fault; it was an odd twist of fate. "No, it's okay. It's just...weird. This is not what I expected."

She tried to pull herself together while she put the heavy kettle down. Looking over his shoulder, she saw that Seth had gone. She stared at the empty doorway, desire kindling her whole body. Both of them were attractive men, and now she'd inadvertently got herself involved with them both. "This situation is going to take some getting used to."

"I understand that, believe me. " He stroked her shoulder, and she had to resist the urge to move closer and take the physical comfort he offered, trying not to let everything she had told him swamp her. "I'll try to make this as easy as possible for you," he added.

She forced herself to nod, but deep down she knew what she wanted, and she didn't want easy. Which was just as well, because this felt as awkward and complicated as it possibly could be and more.

* * * *

Back off. Don't get involved, Seth told himself.

It was his policy when it came to women and he repeated it to himself as he strode down the hallway, returning to the room where he'd spent the night in order to clear his head. *Get a grip*, he told himself. He'd known she was trouble as soon he'd met her, and yet he couldn't resist. Last night was a mistake, but something about the way she'd looked at him made him lose perspective. It had made him want to taste her and see her lips part in pleasure.

She was different to other women, that's why. She hadn't gone all fluttery-eyed on him. Instead, she'd stood up to him, and for some reason that difference meant he'd lost the ability to resist. "Contrary bastard," he muttered to himself.

The door clicked closed behind him, and he looked around the guest room, remembering how he'd helped his stepfather decorate the place the summer before he'd left for his police training. His old room was at the top of the house, but he hadn't been up to his parents flat because he felt it was best. He had to stay close to the witness at all times. That was his priority. Why did that seem like task and a half, when it included Miss Hotpants?

When he'd caught sight of her talking with Adrian, in broken whispers, so intimate and close, it had been a timely reminder. She was here because she was a secondary witness, and that was because she was involved with Adrian. He'd had no right to get involved, even though she'd kissed him, and it was a big mistake.

He shook his head. He couldn't afford the brainpower to even think about it; he was supposed to be working out a way to expose Emery Lavonne in the safest way possible. He had to let his chief know they had a viper in their nest, but he couldn't put the witness at risk while doing so. It had occurred to him that Lavonne might expose himself, given time. Stephen Ward, their chief, was a clever man. He'd figure out the nature of the reason for the unorthodox behaviour in regard to the witness. It was just a matter of time.

As long as he had the witness safe, that was his primary concern.

Chapter Seven

The witness protection division was in chaos. Emery Lavonne stalked in, using the chaos as cover for the fact he was late. As he did, he caught sight of one of his fellow officers jogging out of Stephen Ward's office, red in the face and carrying a sheaf of papers. The chief was in bad humour, judging by the overriding sense of urgency in the atmosphere and the raised voices. Seth Jones's change of plans wasn't, as he had expected, planned.

"Please don't tell me you're thinking of going in there," Janine, an admin support officer, said as he passed her desk.

He paused. Janine was a good source of information. "Problem?"

"Uhu. Seth Jones has gone walkabout with his witness. Nobody seems to know where he is, and Stephen is in a foul mood."

"Really? Any ideas why Jones has gone off the grid?"

Janine shrugged. "Apparently he wouldn't explain to his partner, just told him to get lost."

"Weird." He peered through the glass frontage of Ward's office and noticed that Seth Jones's partner was in the office with the boss. Stephen Ward was pacing up and down. Ward and Jones had some kind of bond, an old friendship from their early days on the force. Ward would be furious about this.

He took a deep breath and tried to decide whether to stay low profile, or jump into the fray. Whilst sitting in traffic on his way back from the midlands he'd got his annoyance under wraps and was freshly determined to find out the alternate location Seth Jones had used. Entering the fray might be the fastest route to gathering that information. He walked closer, and leaned up against the open door frame, listening.

Stephen Ward looked even more stressed than usual. He had three officers in there. Two of them from the internal investigation division. Ward was issuing instructions, rapid fire. "We need to check with the emergency services, look into any car accident or anything unusual that took place between here and the safe house. We can't rule anything out." Ward's frown deepened. "Other than that, all we can do is wait until he makes contact, and he better have a bloody good explanation for this."

"Anything I can help with?" Lavonne offered.

Ward looked his way and thought about it for a moment. "No. I need you working on your next witness. I had the file sent down yesterday before this kicked off, you need to stick with that case. Janine is organising a safe house for the lead in to the trial. When she gives you the details, do your usual checks on the place. You'll need to be ready for your one-to-one and the witness relocation in five days time."

Lavonne ground his teeth. Five days. He had hoped this task wouldn't drag on past twenty-four hours, but with Jones and the witness on walkabout, who could say how long it would be. The trial wasn't for another thirteen days. Worst-case scenario, Jones could keep the witness hidden until then. He balked at being penned like this.

He glanced at the paperwork on the desk. Were they checking alternate safe houses? Could he find that out by checking the task sheets online? Maybe. If only he could get closer to Ward, and to the men he had working on the whereabouts. He couldn't afford to draw attention to himself though. As that thought crossed his mind he noticed the two plain clothes officers staring his way and he jolted himself out of his thoughts. Nodding to show he understood, he took his leave.

"I'm here if you need me," he said as he went, and headed for his desk.

* * * *

It took the whole day for Lily to finally relax around the two of them, but it finally happened. Adrian watched her walking round the kitchen that evening, trailing her fingers on the surfaces. Seth was watching her too, Adrian knew that. Why wouldn't he, she was beautiful and sexy and rather embarrassed about the whole situation, which made her blush appealingly every now again, her thick, dark eyelashes lowering whenever she did. Was she thinking sexy thoughts, or did she just look that way?

That morning she'd gone back to her room with a handful of books. After lunch she had lingered, before sitting in the lounge area reading, while they watched TV, occasionally making comments on the shows, edging closer to joining them. When Seth had invited them into the kitchen while he made them some dinner, she'd come with them. A barrier had been breached, and Adrian was glad of it. He could tell Seth was, too.

"Beans on toast, this is your idea of dinner?" Lily asked as she watched Seth pulling provisions out of the box he'd brought from the car.

"You have a problem with that?"

She shrugged at him. "I suppose it makes a change from boring old cheese and pickle sandwiches."

Adrian smiled inwardly. Seth did seem to have a limited range.

Seth rooted about in the box as if he was hoping a three course dinner would materialise, and Lily began opening cupboards, investigating. A moment later she opened a door in the corner of the room and poked her head inside. From what Adrian could see from his seated position, it looked like some kind of larder.

"Hey, why are we eating butties and beans on toast when there is much more interesting stuff in the storeroom in here?"

"There is?" Seth frowned. "The stores are usually cleared out during the winter."

"Well, the shelves aren't full, but there are plenty of dry provisions, pasta and the like, spices. There are some onions and potatoes on the veggie rack, and a whole slew of canned food. I could rustle us up a good meal from what there is." She glanced back over her shoulder. So long as you like Italian." She looked from one to the other of them. "Is Italian good?"

They nodded in unison and she started to carry various items out to the work surface.

"This is better for me than sitting around. It feels more like normal day now I'm in the kitchen."

"You're a cook?" Seth asked.

"Not quite. I run a sandwich shop with my business partner, Andrea." She pointed at him with a large spoon. "And you won't find us boring people to death with cheese and pickle sandwiches."

He gave her a knowing look. "One of these fancy schmancy sandwiches shops?"

"Yup. We call it The Sandwich Boutique. You can have just about any combination of ingredients imaginable."

"The Sandwich Boutique," Seth repeated, and laughed. "Boy, I've heard it all now."

"What's your problem?" she responded.

"No problem." He held his hands up, faking surrender even while he sparred on. "As you so rightly pointed out, I'm not at all skilled in the realms of designer sandwiches."

"Yeah, what would you know?" She smiled as she turned away.

Adrian liked how this felt. The atmosphere was so much more chilled than it had been.

Seth watched her preparing ingredients, then quizzed her some more, tossing a tin of tomato puree in one hand, hanging close by her as she chopped onions. "I thought you said you were a nurse."

She swiped the tin away from his reach. "You're a very suspicious man. I said I *was* a nurse, not any more."

Seth shrugged. "It's my job to be suspicious."

She didn't add to her comment. Adrian shifted in his seat, turning fully towards them. "Lucky for me you used to be a nurse, and lucky for both of us you know how to cook."

"Keep that leg elevated, AW." She issued the instruction then looked at him quickly when she realised she'd called him AW.

Adrian held her gaze, and smiled. She still thought of him by his net handle. That pleased him, because he still thought of her as his *Laidbacklady*. She returned his smile, tentatively, and then she leaned against the counter top and crossed her legs at the ankle. As she did, he could see her brushing her thighs together, what with that short skirt of hers. Her heels were high, too, and it was a damn sexy look.

This was what she'd worn to meet him, he realised.

This sexy outfit that made her look so curvy and leggy and gorgeous. He stared at the line where the skirt ended, his cock hardening, because all of a sudden all he could think about was her sliding her hand between those soft, pale thighs, and touching herself with her fingers—just like she had done when he'd asked her to all those other times.

When he looked up, she was staring at him intently, and she knew exactly what he was thinking about, he could tell. He could also tell that she was aroused. From the rapid rise and fall of her breasts inside that close fitting top to the bright, focused look in her eyes, all the clues were there. If it hadn't been for the fact that Seth asked her a question just at that moment, and she had turned away to answer him, Adrian would have had to fight the urge to request that she walk over, nice and slow, and sit in his lap.

He could have watched her all night. So many times he'd thought about her, wondered what she'd be like, and now—because of the situation—he was getting time to sit back and learn about her, for real. She wasn't what he'd expected, but then he hadn't known, hadn't dared to think about it too much. It had been a bit of fun, and he'd been half expecting her to stand him up. Perhaps that's why he'd overlooked it. Even though he regretted her being pulled into this, there was a part of him that was glad she was here. It took a huge percentage of unpleasantness out off the situation. He'd expected her to be sexy, and she was. For minutes at a time he was able to forget that he was going to stand up and point his finger at a criminal— and that he had a crazy man with gun after him as a result—because of Lily's presence.

Even the way she leaned across the work surfaces to reach for a chopping board was a seduction in motion, as if she would make a natural dancer. That's what she'd wanted, to be a private dancer. The thought lingered in his mind as he watched her lean into a cupboard and lift out serving bowls.

"You okay with plenty of garlic?" she asked, a moment later.

"As long as you are." He winked. He couldn't help flirting with her.

"Cheeky," she whispered, glancing at the door where Seth had disappeared off to moments before. Her expression was filled with warmth though, and when she turned back to the work surface, she glanced back over her shoulder, smiling his way. She was enjoying their connection, even if she was a bit self conscious about it around Seth. He couldn't blame her for that.

"Am I like you imagined I would be?" She delivered the question nonchalantly, lowering her eyelids, but she wanted to know, he could tell.

He smiled. "Not at all."

Her face fell.

"Don't take that badly. You are everything and more than I imagined, and believe me, I had some pretty top-notch imaginings."

Her smile had retuned, and that pleased him. "Your chat was more confident. You're a little more cautious. A little…" He couldn't quite find the right words.

She nodded, a thoughtful look taking up residence on her pretty face. "I know what you mean. It's easy to be more confident online than it is in real life."

"It's still a real person, at the end of the line, a real person's emotions." He was testing the water with her.

"Yes, and that's the scary part." She continued with her chopping.

Didn't she want to talk about it any more? He couldn't tell, but the kitchen activities seemed to settle her, and a moment later she began to hum while she cooked. That sound undid a knot between his shoulders blades, relieving a huge amount of tension. He'd been worrying about her, but she was doing okay.

"Is merlot good for you guys?" Seth was back, and he'd brought wine, several bottles.

"It's good for me," Adrian said, wondering if it would take the edge off the pain in his leg. The regular painkillers Seth had found had barely touched it. He needed anti-inflammatories, but he hated to ask. It seemed like these two were doing so much for him already; and he didn't want to be a nuisance.

"Ooh, yes, that'll be perfect," Lily responded, nodding at his choice of wine.

It was good to see her more relaxed with both of them.

Later, when she'd served the food and the wine had been opened, they gathered the tall stools around one end of the breakfast bar and sat down together, properly, for the first tine.

Seth lifted his glass, raising a toast. "To good food and grand company, whatever the circumstances of our arrival here."

Adrian chinked his glass and then Lily's, repeating the toast.

"Yes, to all of that." Her cheeks warmed. She was at home now; it was as if the cooking had grounded her. When she met Adrian's gaze, her smile made something deep inside him feel rich and pleasured. He liked her, a lot. And he was getting hard. That smile held such erotic promise. He wondered if she was aware of it.

"How long have you been doing this job?" she asked Seth during the meal.

"I've been in the force all my adult life. In witness protection..." he paused, as if counting back, "six years."

"That's got to be tough, I mean, being away from home as much as you are." She frowned.

"Home is where my job is."

"It has to be, I guess," Adrian added, thinking aloud. "But this place is great, much more comfortable than I expected."

Seth's smile was tense, and he didn't respond. Adrian recalled it was a last minute change of location.

"Yes," Lily agreed, "I was thinking that, it's like a retreat, beautiful countryside, too."

Seth nodded. "This is great pasta."

Had he changed the topic of conversation on purpose? It seemed so, because he changed it again.

"So, you two...you met online. In a chat room, yes?" He forked another mouthful of pasta into his mouth.

Adrian had a bad feeling. This felt like bloke-talk. How would Lily react?

She stared at Seth, her fork frozen in her hand. "You're trying to embarrass me."

"No, not at all." Seth looked much more relaxed than Lily did. He pointed his fork at her, briefly. "You've got to lighten up, Miss Hotpants."

"Bloody hell," she muttered, her face colouring.

Tension arced through the atmosphere between them, Adrian couldn't help noticing it. He also noticed what Seth had called her. Hotpants. Did Seth fancy her? He'd be a fool not to, Adrian surmised, wryly. And now Lily was looking at the cop from under he lashes, her lower lip caught between her teeth in a really sexy way. Did she want Seth? He considered the question and quickly swallowed down his rising annoyance. He couldn't blame her for gravitating towards the bloke who was taking care of them both. All he'd done was get her mixed up in his problems. If that meant she changed her mind about their set up, he'd have to take it as righteous payoff, like it or not.

Seth scooped more pasta to one side of the bowl before he continued speaking. "Like I said before, I'm just trying to make you relax. It's really not a problem."

"Not a problem?" Her eyes rounded. Adrian had stopped eating, observing the exchange with deepening curiosity and concern. She was focused on Seth; she definitely liked him, that electric heat she was giving off told him that—it wasn't just annoyance.

Seth shook his head, real slow. "Lily, listen to me, please. The reason you two met is like an elephant in the room. We are all aware of the elephant, but no one wants to mention it." He paused, his lips pressed together as if deep in thought, before he continued. "Trust me; we need to get the conversation over with."

Did they? Adrian wasn't so sure. Maybe Lily had changed her mind and this was forcing her to think about it again. Seth adopted a relaxed position, bowl in one hand. Did he learn how to deal with this kind of stuff for his job, Adrian wondered. Whether he did or not, it was a good approach, because although he was in charge and he was addressing a potentially uncomfortable subject with Lily, his body language was all about being chilled and non-confrontational.

Even so, Lily looked agitated. Putting down her fork, she pushed back her hair then folded her arms across her chest, elbows on the table. "Whatever. I can't eat now."

Adrian felt bad for her. He reached out one hand and touched her briefly on the arm. She gave him a grateful smile.

"Seth, is this really necessary?" Adrian quizzed. "Lily and I are old online friends, that's all that matters here."

Seth nodded his way. "Lily has to understand that I'm forthright, but it's meant in an entirely genuine way." He shrugged. "I'm not the bad guy here, and she has to stop thinking that."

Lily rested her elbows on the table, her forehead in her hands. "I know. You're not."

She wriggled her shoulders as if she couldn't let that one go, but Adrian felt the tension dissipate, marginally. Did she need someone to blame? If so, she should be blaming him, it was all his fault. Adrian sent Seth a pleading glance.

Seth nodded, connecting, before he commented any further. "The reason you two met doesn't have to be a big deal, really. Did you know that a large percentage of happy long term couples meet online these days?"

Adrian was surprised. "Seriously?" He glanced at Lily. She was still tense, but she was listening. "It's not that unusual?"

Seth replied. "No."

"How do you know that?" Lily picked up her fork again as she directed the question at him, lightening up a bit, but still quite obviously mistrustful of Seth's line of conversation. Whatever the reason for her caution on the matter, Adrian liked the feeling it gave him — that she was protective of what they had. Did he still have a chance with her? What they already had was special, and it hung in the balance right now, in danger of not moving forward.

Seth smiled across the table at them both. "In a job like mine you sometimes have hours on end to read magazines."

Adrian took his chance to agree. "You're right. It isn't a big deal."

Lily sat still for the longest moment, and then she took a deep breath and stood up. "Maybe not, but I don't want to talk about it right now." She stared Seth's way. "Because it's, well...it's complicated. You know why."

This was still embarrassing her, Adrian realised. He didn't want anything to make her feel uncomfortable. He reached out and brushed his fingers down her arm, eager to connect.

"Okay," Seth responded quickly. "It doesn't have to be 'complicated'. Neither of us wants you to feel that way."

He looked at Adrian, and Adrian nodded. Lily's gaze covered them both, watchful and intelligent.

"Let it go." Seth stood up, picking his fork and bowl in one hand as he did so. "Let's go watch a DVD."

Lily stared at him.

"This is really good," he added, gesturing with the bowl of pasta in his hand. "Much better than anything I could conjure up." He spanked her on the arse with his free hand as he passed.

Her mouth fell open. Adrian couldn't help chuckling.

When Lily looked at him, questioningly, he shrugged at her and then picked up his bowl in one hand and limped after Seth, leaning on his stick with his other hand. Seth was trying to diffuse the tension, and she was coming round. Adrian wasn't going to argue with that. Hope could be a hellish burden sometimes, he reflected. *Follow us*, he silently pleaded, as he limped away from her, a hot tick in his chest willing her to be okay with this.

Chapter Eight

Lily stood in the doorway of the residents' lounge, hesitant. Adrian had settled into an armchair. Seth had put the music channel on and flicked through a stack of DVDs next to the player. Both of them were half-watching her, silently, expectantly. They wanted her to come in to the room, they wanted her to follow. Something was rising to the surface here — something that felt dangerous and wild — but she couldn't walk away.

Adrian's expression told her he was thinking about what they'd shared, and her bottom still tingled from where Seth had spanked her. Her imagination was roaming from the memory of Seth's blatant sexual response the evening before, to Adrian's online sexual adventuring. All of it fired through her, hot and lusty, alive. Between her thighs, her pulse beat out a frenzied tattoo. All through the meal, the sexual tension between them had ratcheted up, making her keenly aware of both men. If she went in there with them, something would happen. But Seth had a point; she would feel better if it was out in the open. At the moment, it was making her feel awkward, and she could do without that on top of the weirdness of the situation.

Stepping into the room, she tried to act as nonchalantly as she could. She pulled a footstool in front of Adrian, encouraging him to put his leg up.

"You're right," she said casually, glancing at Seth.

Seth immediately stopped what he was doing to listen.

"It would be much easier if I got it out into the open."

He abandoned the DVDs and left the music channel playing on the TV instead. Moving to the sofa, he sat easily on one end, his attention apparently all hers.

Oh boy. Taking a deep breath, she took the opposite end of the sofa to him, placing herself closer to Adrian in his armchair. Adrian looked as if he approved of what she had said, which gave her strength.

"I don't want us to feel awkward anymore." She directed her attention to Seth. "Adrian I have been chatting online for about three months. Things got pretty steamy." That felt like the understatement of the century, but considering what had happened with Seth the night before, she was pretty sure she didn't need to go into more detail. He could figure it out for himself.

He looked as if he was trying to remain serious and inscrutable, and yet there was a simmering sense of expectation about him and a dark twinkle in his eyes. Bastard. He thought it was funny.

She took a deep breath and continued. "Yesterday was supposed be our first meeting in person. Adrian was very kind and suggested that I go to his office so that I would feel safe, in a public place. So you see, this is all feels a bit awkward because Adrian and I know a lot about each other, but we don't really *know* each other." She paused. "The deal was that I could walk away, and so could he, if we didn't feel comfortable during our date. Without even having had any time to get past that first meeting, we're locked up together. With you."

It felt good to have said it out loud, for the first time.

"I can see why that would be difficult, of course," Seth commented, in a very matter of fact way. "That's it, out in the open, over with. It wasn't so hard now, was it?"

She dipped her head on one side as she looked at him, considering why he had said that. He gave her a brief smile and rested one elbow on the back of sofa. Maybe he didn't want her to say anything else, or maybe he was suggesting she did? Whatever, she was on a roll and she wasn't stopping now, because as far as she was concerned she'd only got halfway through the problem. "There's something else that I want to get off my chest, as well."

Thank God for the wine. It didn't exactly make her throw caution to the wind, but it made this a hell of a lot easier to get this off her chest. Forcing herself to glance at both of them, she quickly took in their expressions. Adrian was curious, and Seth looked bemused. His eyebrows had lifted imperceptibly, those sharp eyes totally focused on her. Oh yes, he knew what she was about to say, he'd guessed. Was there a touch of admiration there? Maybe. Maybe this is what he'd been pushing for all along.

She turned to Adrian. "When I arrived at your office, I thought...well, I thought you would answer the door, and that you had in fact answered the door. So I...kissed you." Now it was Adrian's eyebrows that lifted. "I mean, I kissed him." Nodding her head in Seth's direction, she barely dared look at him.

Would Seth laugh at her? Would Adrian hate her? She hoped not.

The sound of the music from the TV only seemed to emphasise the silence that hung in the atmosphere. Adrian stared at her for what seemed an age, and she had to fight the urge to squirm in her seat or flee from the room. Then he shook his head, a wry half-smile taking up residence on his face. "Well, that explains a lot."

She stared at him, unsure of how to respond.

He nodded at Seth. "The way you look at Lily. It was more than just casual interest, now I see why."

Seth lifted his hands. "Sorry, buddy."

Adrian kept staring from one to the other of them, his eyes flickering with curiosity. "Is she a good kisser?"

Lily's skin raced hot and cold, her senses on high alert.

"Hellish hot," Seth responded, watching her in a blatantly assessing way. She suddenly wished she hadn't sat on the same sofa as him. His proximity made this even worse, and she had to force herself to breathe. He smiled a lopsided grin that made her think he was referring just as much to what happened between them last night, as in London.

Lily's face burned, and that wasn't all. Between her legs her pussy felt hot and heavy, the pulse at her core beating wildly, a frantic need for contact controlling it. "This is embarrassing," she muttered to herself.

"Hey, don't be embarrassed, *Laidbacklady*, no need. You're a sexy woman."

"It was a genuine mistake," Seth commented.

Adrian shot him a glance. "I'm sure it was, and I don't blame you for enjoying it." His mouth tightened for a moment, thoughtful. "You did enjoy it, right?"

Seth nodded.

"Of course you did. You'd be an idiot not to." Adrian knocked back some more wine before he continued. "But if you're going to snog my sex-chat buddy, the least you can do is let me watch."

Did he really just say that? Lily stared at him. Had he had too much wine?

"You'd like that," he added, "wouldn't you, Lily?" He looked straight at her, his smile knowing and darkly suggestive.

She saw it in his eyes, the secret knowledge he had about her. She had confessed about wanting to be watched, and now he was calling her on it. *Really* calling her. Her mind raced. Was this actually happening to her? Did Adrian honestly want to watch her with another man?

One look at his suggestive smile left her in no doubt that he meant it, and the combination of shock and dynamite arousal she experienced made her feel dizzy on the subsequent rush. Disbelieving but wildly aroused, she shifted restlessly and ran her fingernails over her upper arms, needing the sting to make her breathe.

Seth's soft laughter drew her attention back. The suggestive smile he wore made her shiver with arousal, her body moving rapidly towards total meltdown. "Lily would like that, huh?" Seth put his glass aside. "You two really are into the sex chat."

Before she had a chance to respond, he reached out across the length of the sofa, breaching the space between them, and put his hand on hers. Weaving their fingers together, he drew her towards him, forcing her to move in his direction. Lily's heart hammered in her chest.

Seth paused, his face inches from hers. "You know the lady so well, Adrian, and knowledge is power."

Adrian laughed softly. "It is indeed."

Seth glanced sideways at Adrian again, eyes glittering. "Here's the deal. I'll let you watch, if you share what you know."

Lily whimpered, his words shocking her, desire and tension making her feel strung out. Every part of her was wired to their exchange in the most direct way, her nerve endings sparking.

With one hand, Seth stroked her hair back from her face, cupping her cheek. "Tell me everything she likes, I want to know it all."

"Well now, Lily did seem to like it when I told her I'd stand between her legs and tell her to touch herself."

Lily bit her lip, and squirmed in her seat. Hearing Adrian say it aloud, the thing that had turned her on so much—and that no man had ever done—was a whole other level of torment.

"I also told her that I would watch her while she did it, and that would really turn her on."

Adrian seemed determined to push this thing forward. Meanwhile Seth's proximity only served to remind her how it had felt to be pressed against him, to feel that persuasive mouth on hers. At her centre, she ached for that—and more.

"Is that true?" Seth's eyes were dark with arousal, hooded and intense. He stared at her lips as he spoke, and when she eventually nodded at him he lowered his head to hers.

Any resistance she might have felt faded when he pushed his fingers into her hair and eased her back against the cushions, his body covering hers. Possessively, he claimed her, his kiss long and hungry, his mouth moving on hers, opening her up. Latching her hands over his shoulders her body arched up to his. The physical contact was too good, and all the while the heat of Adrian's eyes on them seemed to make everything that much more intense, adding a thousand more caresses to each of Seth's.

"Oh yes," Adrian said, his voice low and hoarse, "you're so beautiful. The way you're moving makes me hard." He sighed, and Seth's hands moved over her, stroking her throat and her breasts before wrapping around her waist, claiming her. At the same time it was Adrian's voice she heard, and it seemed to coil inside her and flare, making her open and melt, the physical need that gripped her multiplying.

Seth lifted his head, but his hands were still locked around her waist. He'd pinned her on the sofa by sitting against her hip and locking her in place, and now he was leaning over her and looking at her with those suggestive eyes, kissing her until she was desperate with need.

I want you, she thought. *Heaven help me, I want you both.* She pressed back into the cushions, desire and self-awareness washing over her in equal measures.

Seth touched her mouth with one finger, outlining it. "I'm going to explore you some more now, and unless you say otherwise, Adrian is going to watch exactly what I'm doing."

Lily gripped Seth's shoulders with her hands, unable to look away from him.

"Watching is the least you can offer, seeing as you're stealing my date here." Adrian laughed softly, a self-deprecating tone to his comment.

"Stealing? And there was me thinking we were sharing." Seth smiled, a weighty message in his voice and his expression. "Your call, Lily," he added, and his expression softened for a moment. He'd made his deal with Adrian, but he still wanted her okay on it.

Lily couldn't respond. The idea of being watched while this moved forward made her crazy, and one glance assured her that both men wanted it. As if in query, Seth moved the back of his hand down the front of her skirt, making fleeting contact with the mound of her pussy through the fabric. It was tantalising and tempting and delicious.

From the corner of her eye, she saw Adrian move in his armchair. "Who knew this would be a chance for you to live out some of those things you confessed in the chat room?"

Embarrassment quickly multiplied inside her, her own words coming back to haunt her—words that she had typed to him in their private chat room when she was high on the rush from anonymous confession and the heavy arousal that followed. "Adrian. You've had too much to drink," she blurted.

"Loosed my tongue, hmm, that what you think? Hey, don't fight it, gorgeous. Right now you look like every bloke's wet dream come true, and I for one am loving the view."

She squirmed and rolled her head on the cushions, the back of her wrist against her forehead. Seth eased her skirt up around her hips and cupped the mound of her pussy through her knickers.

"You said you wanted this," Adrian added, concern had edged into his tone.

"I did, but I didn't mean like this," she said, and the words came out in a sudden rush that betrayed her state of arousal.

"It's making you hot though, this way? With the two of us here," Seth asked.

"Of course it is," she blurted, incredulous. She sighed ruefully. Her body was lost to the moment, her body on fire at Seth's touches, her mind recalling all the things she had said to Adrian and his comments egging her on to display her sexuality.

Seth smiled and ran one hand over her breasts, making her moan. "We could stop this, but you seem to be enjoying it, and — like Adrian said — you're every bloke's wet dream right now, so neither of us is complaining."

No, she didn't want to stop, but the words wouldn't form.

Her hips rocked up against his hand, and that was enough. He pulled down her knickers, drawing them the length of her thighs, and she lifted and shifted to aid him. When the barrier was gone, he bent to kiss her mouth again, and at the very same moment he moved his hand between her thighs and pushed one finger into her slit, brushing it over her swollen clit.

Moaning against his mouth, Lily couldn't help herself. Her hips lifted, her hands closing around his head. Moving her fingers against his thick hair, she savoured the feeling of it while she opened her mouth to take him in, her tongue moving with his in the dance of seduction. Between her thighs, he applied more pressure to her clit and then moved his finger, tantalisingly. Her sex clenched, clamping where she wanted to feel him hard and thrusting and rhythmic inside her.

Would Adrian be turned on by that? Would he want to be inside her as well? The questions rushed her mind, sidelining her. She pulled back, gasped for breath. "Oh, oh,"

Seth's face was shadowed, the light beyond him, but she saw his eyes flicker and he laughed softly. Again he moved his fingers against her pussy, making her cry out, her fingernails sinking deep into his shoulders. His shoulders lifted in response and he growled. "Fuck this, let me at you."

Kneeling on the floor beside the sofa, he shifted her bodily; turning her so that she sat upright, then he stroked both legs from thigh to ankle — an action that did nothing to ground her — before pushing both legs apart, and ducking his head between them as he went down on her. His hands worked her thighs, stroking their soft insides, making her tremble, while his mouth worked pure magic. Knotting her fingers together, Lily's arms shot up, then bent at the elbow and dropped behind her head, her body arching from the sofa , her breasts jutting as his mouth closed over her clit. First he sucked her clit until she about lifted off the seat, then he explored her hot, swollen folds with his tongue until she cried aloud and bit the back of her wrist when she heard herself.

"That is so hot," Adrian whispered, and she forced herself to look his way. He was sitting forward in his chair, watching avidly. His eyes were bright and what she saw there was something akin to pride. He liked this, he really did.

That pushed her to the edge, and she ran her fingers into Seth's hair, her clit painfully tender as she blossomed and climaxed. Heat washed over her and her free hand went to her throat, where she seemed to burn. Panting, she rolled her hips, her thighs trembling. When she surfaced, she found that Seth was busy taking off her shoes.

He's not done with me yet. The realisation hit her; Seth was just warming her up.

Smiling wickedly, he stood up. Clasping her hand in his, he drew her to her feet. Then he reached into his pocket, pulled out his wallet, and extracted a condom packet. When she looked at it, then at him, he flickered his eyebrows at her and threw the condom packet onto the sofa so that it was within easy reach. Her groin was still buzzing, the ache at her core up and raring for that condom to be put into action. With his hands firm and decisive on her upper arms, Seth turned her to face Adrian, and then pulled her top up and over her head, undressing her in front of her virtual lover.

"Oh boy," she murmured, her legs wavering under her. On the TV, a rolling drum and guitar frenzy echoed her racing pulse with uncanny accuracy. Glancing down at where Adrian sat in the armchair, she saw that he was hard inside the jeans we wore, his zipper bulging. She had longed to see his cock; she'd thought about it so often while she made herself come. Was that the way he looked when they were chatting online? Did he stroke his cock while he urged her to pleasure herself? When she met his gaze, she could tell he knew what was in her mind. His gaze lowered to her chest, where Seth was busy undoing her sheer black bra. When he unhooked it and pulled it free, her cheeks flamed, her hands going to cover her bare breasts.

"Uh oh, no hiding, not now." Adrian shook his finger at her, still smiling.

She moved her fingers away. He was right; there was no going back now.

Her nipples were rock hard, her breasts swollen and uplifted. Exposing them felt outrageously good. Between her thighs, she was damp and sticky from her orgasm. At her back, Seth spooned her hips, moving in time to the rock music, shifting first one way, then the other, taking her with him. His cock was rock hard. She felt it through his jeans and the thin layer of her mini skirt, the only item she still wore. His free hand was at her nape, stoking her hair out of his way. He rested a kiss on her hot skin, his mouth soft, the stubble of his chin brusque and vivid on her sensitised skin. She felt shaky and high all the same time, delirious with pleasure as she absorbed the sheer amount of testosterone in the atmosphere and thought about what was coming. It was heavy in the air, expectancy, the thrill of knowing it was going all the way.

A moment later, Seth unzipped the skirt and peeled it off her. "Crazy lady, you have us both in such a state."

"You're doing this," she murmured, as he shoved the skirt down her hips and let it drop to the floor.

Adrian shook his head, reaching out to stroke her legs when Seth danced her closer, his fingers lingering around the back of her knee. "No, you are, you're doing it all, and it's everything you wanted."

It was true, but this was also beyond her fantasies. Way beyond. She hadn't even thought about having two men before. This was overdose, had to be, she was sure of it. Moaning, she tried to turn her face into Seth's chest, but he tutted mockingly and then he lifted her hair from the back of a neck and kissed her there again. He was making her face up to Adrian, her secret online lover, and that was so arousing—and so true to what she'd wanted, deep down—that instinct took over.

She knew what she wanted.

Bending over, she undid Adrian's belt and lowered his zipper. His cock poked up through his jockey shorts and when she ran a hand over its outline through the soft cotton, his hands tightened on the arms of his chair, knuckles turning white. There was a warning in his eyes.

Seth squeezed her hips with hands, his erection pressing against her bottom suggestively. "Are you going to go down on him?"

She nodded. It was what she wanted to do, and he knew that, but he was also letting her know that he wasn't going to be left out. If she went down on Adrian, she was still going to get him. Both of them. Could she handle it? Her heart hammered wildly, her body high on the idea of it, adrenaline rushing in her veins.

Dropping to her knees, she pulled Adrian's cock free of his jockey shorts. Free of its constraint, it bounced into her hand, eager for her touch. The skin was hot, the shaft hard. She stroked her fingers over its swollen head. It made her shiver inside. Wrapping her hands around its solid shaft, she licked the head and then took it into her mouth, savouring the hot, saltiness of it on her tongue.

Seth had knelt down behind her and his hands were on her hips. She concentrated on Adrian's cock, denying the self-consciousness that rose when she realised she was so thoroughly on display to Seth.

Then she heard the sound of his zipper, and she forgot to be embarrassed.

A moment later, the sound of a condom packet being opened. When the thick, blunt head of his cock moved up and down the niche of her sex, sliding easily again her wet skin, her bottom lifted, her pussy reaching and clutching, desperately needy for him inside. He eased into her, and she opened readily. With one hand on the base of her spine, he edged deeper inside her, inch by inch. His cock was gloriously hard, and as he filled her with it, it sent sensations spinning through her entire body. His legs enclosed hers as he moved into position, stretching the walls of her sex to accommodate the length and girth of his erection, his crown buried deep inside her.

Lifting her head, she moaned and panted, her hands still wrapped around Adrian's cock as she rode it up and down. Adrian's eyes burned with intensity. Reaching in to her face, he lifted a stray hair away from her cheek with one finger.

Seth's hands moved under her chest, cupping her breasts from behind. She felt totally enclosed by him, and when he drew back and thrust, she squeezed Adrian's cock and took it back into her mouth, moving in time to the deep, rhythmic thrust of Seth's cock inside her. Locked between the two of them, she felt part anchor, part chain—wholly strung out and awash with pleasure as she took everything they had to give. And Seth had plenty to give.

He thrust deep, riding her rhythmically. One hand stroked her spine almost tenderly as his cock plunged in and out of her hungry sex. She clutched, and Seth moaned aloud, and she took Adrian's cock deeper, running it against the roof of her mouth. She heard one of them curse but was lost to the moment, bound into both of them in that moment of extreme mutual pleasure.

Then Adrian lifted her chin, easing her away. "I'm going to come," he said, his free hand on his cock pumping it quickly. Rebelling, she licked the head, and he spurted against her mouth and chin. His climax triggered an instant reaction, her pussy clamping on the cock inside her.

"So am I." It was Seth, and he thrust faster still, the head of his cock rubbing brusquely over her sensitised centre.

Her sex clutched, released, and clutched again, her orgasm closing. "Oh."

Her eyelids flickered up when Adrian's hand under her chin forced her to look at him again as she reached her peak, making her live her wildest fantasies.

"Let me see you," he whispered.

Tossing back her hair, she moaned aloud, almost there.

Seth's cock jerked. His fingers tightened on her buttocks, making her crazy.

Her hips reached, thrusting up to meet his, her body burning up as her sex went into spasm, her release so intense that she shuffled on her knees and gripped onto Adrian's thighs with her hands.

Crying aloud, her hips ground against Seth's as her core spasmed again and again, spinning her out of control until the peak hit and then burst through her in dizzy waves of release.

Chapter Nine

Lily awoke into struggling winter sunlight. It spilled into the bedroom through badly drawn curtains. She blinked into it, shielded her eyes, and realised that she was being watched. Adrian was lying alongside her, propped up on one elbow. He smiled down at her as she woke and then stroked his hand over her shoulder, as if he'd been waiting to do that for some time. "Good morning, sleepyhead."

"Good morning, AW."

His eyes lit when she called him AW, and he bent to rest a gentle kiss on her shoulder. "You have the most beautiful shoulders."

She couldn't have quelled the smile that hit her at that moment, not if her life had depended on it. He had stubble on his chin and the light glinted off the golden hairs dotted here and there. His hair looked so much lighter with the bit of sun behind him, and she noticed how unusual his eyes were, hazel, truly green flecked with brown, like freckles. "Beautiful shoulders, huh?"

"Beautiful everything." He stroked her hair back from her face before returning his hand to her arm.

She chuckled and stirred beneath the duvet. Her legs were tangled with his, and when she moved, his hand stilled on her shoulder and he squeezed her. She rested a hand against his chest, where he was warm and inviting. Desire blossomed inside her, warm and vibrant and needy. The urge to snuggle closer stole over her. *Where is Seth?*

Glancing back over her shoulder, she saw there was a space on the bed, where Seth had been throughout the night.

"He's gone to make breakfast." Adrian commented.

Blinking again, she took in her surroundings. "The winter light seems so different out here."

"The trees are bare, and we're used to the city. There aren't any other buildings nearby."

She nodded. "It's a real retreat." The room was similarly decorated to her own, but larger. "Whose room is this?" When she turned to look at him again, he ran one finger down from her forehead to the tip of her nose and then touched her briefly on the lips.

"You don't remember?" There was a teasing tone to his voice.

"I was being distracted by two rather demanding men when we made it in here."

"It's my room. Seth thought the double bed would help with the leg, give me a bit more room to stretch out."

"Oh, yes. Is it okay?" She drew away from him, aware that she could be rather close to his knee with hers, but he grabbed her when she moved and held onto her, urging her not to pull away.

"It's fine. It only hurts when I put my weight on it. Besides, after last night, I don't feel any pain any more."

His eyes flickered, and he looked at her with a meaningful stare.

Her body heated up even faster as she thought about what she'd done, how she'd been with them both. "Oh, really."

"You were incredible."

"Is that a good thing, or a bad thing?" Even though the look in his eyes warmed her right through, she still needed to be sure on that point.

He grinned. "A good thing, oh yes."

Relief ran over her, fast merging with the desire she felt. All the words they had exchanged flitted through her memory, alongside her hopes and fears about meeting him. "We did end up in bed together. I'm so glad." Her fingers found their way to his chest. "You did the most amazing things to me when were chatting online. It was like you knew all the right things to say."

"Luck."

She shook her head. "You made me feel so alive. I'll never forget that."

"I'll never forget it either...or this." He leant in and kissed her, his mouth brushing over hers so tantalisingly, so inquisitively, that her hand instinctively stole around his neck, drawing him closer and opening them both up to it. He responded by tangling his fingers in her hair, locking her to the moment. It made her melt into him, her hands learning him, her body arching to brush against his while it lasted and lasted.

"Longed to do that," he murmured hoarsely when they drew apart, and she realised they hadn't kissed properly before.

He inhaled deeply and stretched happily, like a man reprieved. Stunned, Lily eyed him, admiring him. He was fit—not muscular like Seth was, but lean and wiry like a long distance runner—and there was a welcome tinge of amusement glinting in his expression since the night before. He was so much more relaxed than he had been.

That meant it was a good thing, right? Doubts assailed her. This experience was like nothing that had ever happened to her before, in so many ways. Last night's action had been out of the blue, and whilst it had felt right at the time she wasn't so sure now and felt horribly insecure about it. "I didn't think it would happen the way it did, I must confess."

She wanted to know if he was upset about Seth's involvement.

"Sometimes you just have to go with the flow." He pursed his lips, then shifted and shook his head, rolling his eyes. "You were so bloody hot."

Pleasure burned in her, and she wriggled against him. "No I wasn't!"

"You were. I wanted you, always wanted you, but when I came round and I saw you leaning over me, wow. And then my bloody leg gave out. Just as well Seth was there to pick up the slack and show you a good time. I couldn't have made you that happy on my own."

Lily was amazed. Did he really think that? "Men!"

"Men what?"

"Always thinking of the physical practicalities."

"Yeah. We have to keep our end up, keep the ladies happy." He was smiling and he toyed with her hair while she snuggled against his shoulder on the pillow. "I have to say I feel a hell of a lot less guilty about you being stuck here now, because you enjoyed yourself so much last night."

Was that why? Guilt?

"Please don't feel guilty. This situation wasn't anything you did on purpose, but you're right, last night was special." She sighed loudly. "Thing is, Seth forced us to break the ice. It was hard to get it out in the open. How difficult would it have been for just the two of us?"

"We'll never know."

She glanced back at him, unsure. "You really didn't feel bad about Seth getting involved? I did think he was you when I kissed him, back in London."

He studied her intently before he replied. What did that mean? Guilt stole into her heart again, making it ache. She didn't plan it, not any of it. It just happened that way, and he had encouraged it, after all. If anyone pushed it along, it was him. But maybe he was reacting to what she'd said, and regretted that now? Either way, she didn't want him to feel slighted in any way. She liked him, a lot. A heck of a lot.

"Lily, stop fretting. I wouldn't change last night for the world. To be able to see you like that and learn how you like to be touched, and then what you did, the way you went down on me...you blew my head off, lady."

She caught her bottom lip between her teeth, unsure how to respond. The truth of it was she had got carried away on the moment, on the dynamic between the three of them. Adrian had pressed all the right buttons, and Seth had played into it without reserve. Unleashed, her libido had rolled with every delicious moment.

"I kept thinking you'd do a runner when you met me," Adrian continued. "In fact it's kind of fortuitous for me that you can't actually leave," he teased.

"AW, you're even more devious than I thought you were."

He winked. "Yeah, well, it obviously takes two men to handle a woman like you."

She prodded him in the chest with one finger. "Not at all. That was a surprise, if I had just met you, we'd have been fine, I'm sure we would."

"You think so?" Curiosity mixed with the humour in his eyes. He obviously didn't believe her, but he seemed quite chilled with the Seth angle.

"I think so." Their eyes locked, and something unfurled inside her, that thing she hadn't dared think about too much when she'd gone to meet him. She could grow to care for this man, deeply. On the surface he was so level-headed, and yet that hidden streak revealed itself when she was already throwing caution to the wind. How could he make her feel safe and yet out of control at the very same time?

"You pushed me on last night, you can't deny that."

"I'm not trying to deny it. It was the best thing in the world, especially after all that...waiting, the perpetual hard-ons you gave me."

That comment made her smile, it also made her damp. Her clit ticked restlessly, and she knew she was getting wet. The urge to climb onto him and join them together was rising, but she also wanted to hear everything he had to say, now that the barriers were down.

He lifted her hand from his chest, and kissed her palm. "Thank you, for everything you did." He pointed at his knee and his head. "That too."

She shook her head, feeling as if she owed him so much more. The night before he'd unlocked her somehow, unlocked something that she couldn't have managed on her own, something that made her feel so much more sexually aware and confident.

"You saved my life," he added, growing serious.

"Don't be daft."

"You did. I'd found my diary on my desk, and when I realised it was you, I dropped it. I bent to pick it up just as that goon took a shot at me."

"No," she whispered. "I don't believe it."

"It's true. If we hadn't arranged to meet, I might not be alive right now."

"Hush." She was getting upset about the fact he'd been so easily targeted. "There's no need to thank me for anything, really."

His eyes seemed to darken, and she felt the tension stirring in him — tension that was echoed inside her. The door creaked open. Lily had to drag her attention away. A moment longer and they would have been making love.

"Breakfast is served, such as it is." Seth walked in carrying three steaming mugs in one hand, and a plate piled high with buttered toast in the other. He made the announcement apologetically, and put the breakfast things down on the bedside table nearest Lily. When he glanced at them, he ruffled his hair with one hand, awkwardly.

He knows he interrupted, bless him. She shuffled up in the bed, plumping her pillow behind her with one hand, the other concealing her breasts with the duvet. "Yum, much appreciated. I'm starving."

That's when she noticed that the only thing Seth wore was snug-fitting black jockey shorts. His chest and abs magnetised her attention. They were ripped, tight and firm. Something that felt almost desperate plumed inside her. Lust, she told herself, feeling confused. This threesome thing was good, but so damn weird. A moment before she'd been wrapped in Adrian. Now that Seth was here, she wanted him as well.

He hovered by, as if unsure. "I've ramped the heating up, it's icy out there this morning."

"Come back to bed then," Lily suggested, resisting the urge to reach out for him, picking up a mug of tea instead.

Seth grinned and sat down on the bed, back in the spot he'd vacated earlier. "My God, the woman's insatiable."

"Hey, I meant for you to keep warm." The fact he'd mentioned her sexual appetite seemed to stir it up even more. It also embarrassed her a tad, and she sipped her tea. It was good, and she filched the top piece of toast from the stack, purring audibly as she tucked into it. Adrian followed suit and for a little while they all ate and drank.

"This tea is good, you make a great cuppa."

"I'm glad I meet your approval on something."

"Judging from all that moaning last night," Adrian interjected, "you meet her approval on a lot of things."

Lily couldn't help laughing.

"Glad to be of service, but what I actually meant was in the kitchen department," Seth said, echoing her earlier clarification.

"Oh, right."

He ate his toast silently for a moment, but she could tell he had something on his mind. His eyes grew shuttered and he had that deadly-serious policeman face on. "Tell me more about the bloke you saw outside Adrian's office," he said, eventually.

"More? There isn't much more." She shrugged one shoulder and pulled the duvet higher over her chest before wrapping both hands around the mug of tea. "He was in the elevator with me as I came up. He made me feel uneasy, something about him." She glanced at Adrian. "I got a bit freaked; like, worried that he might be you."

Seth stared at them both. "You really had no clue what each other looked like?"

"Nope," Adrian replied, "That was Lily's call."

She nodded. "I'd rather have no clue than be sent a fake photo."

Seth looked at them dubiously. "Makes sense, I suppose."

"I liked Adrian from his words. It was what he said to me that made me want to meet him." She stroked Adrian's head playfully. "Not just the sexy stuff," she added, when he winked. "You said normal stuff as well, and you made me feel comfortable. That's important to a woman. "

"I'm glad." His voice was barely above a whisper.

"What happened in the elevator?" Seth quizzed, drawing her back to the topic he was focused on, and then drank his tea as he listened.

He really did want to know. Was it important? Had to be. His job was to protect the witness, but she guessed he was reporting back to his colleagues on the blond guy, the 'shooter' as he had previously called him.

"He knew where he was going, or seemed to."

"Probably checked the place out before hand," Seth commented. "He knew the fire escape went around to Adrian's office."

"When he got out of the elevator, he pushed me out of the way. I followed behind, trying to locate the suite. He kept looking back at me, so I lingered outside a door about half way down the corridor. That's when he shot out of the window."

Seth's expression grew overcast.

"I figured he was a maintenance man," she added.

Seth rubbed a hand through his hair, putting his mug down. "You would, of course you would." He gave her a brief smile, but he was deep in thought.

She felt Adrian growing tense again, and wished Seth hadn't gone into it while he was there. "I'm guessing this is pretty heavy stuff, because of the evidence you're giving?"

Adrian nodded.

"What happens next? I mean, how long is it until the trial?"

"Ten days and hopefully Carlisle will be locked up for good. It can't be over soon enough." Adrian looked across at Seth. "Oh, bloody hell...I shouldn't have even said that, should I. Sorry."

"I didn't hear it," she offered, sensing this was difficult for them all.

Seth squeezed her hand. "Good girl."

Adrian had lost his relaxed demeanour, and he stared across at Seth. "Did any of your other witnesses ever regret giving evidence?"

"Just about every one, at one point or another."

"Well, I guess that's reassuring, kind of." He had a faraway look in his eye and he turned away and drank his tea. Lily noticed how browbeaten he looked. No wonder he had overlooked their date. This was heavy stuff.

"It always seems like a long wait," Seth said, "but it'll be behind you soon and you will have no regrets then, believe me."

"I hope you're right."

"Trust me."

The moment was heavy, but it obviously needed to be said. Lily considered that first meeting, how angry Seth had been when he'd almost lost his witness, how much care he'd taken about getting the pair of them out of the building and out of London. After a moment, she flipped open the duvet cover, and invited Seth back into the bed.

Putting his mug down on the floor, he climbed in and spooned her hips with his, his hand moving around her to cup her breast. He nuzzled at the back of her neck before he continued speaking. "The less you know the better. I know that's hard, but it's safest for everyone involved."

"I understand." Lily exhaled, her back tingling as he took up residence against it. He seemed to like planting kisses on the back of her neck, and he breathed against the skin in the most provocative way. That area had never had so much attention, but she wasn't complaining. Apparently it was a sensitive place and it made her respond to him in the most delicious way, sending darts of stimulation all over her, from her nipples to her toes.

Adrian took the cup from her hand and she wriggled further down in the bed. Seth grazed her earlobe softly with his teeth, his breath warm on her skin. Her body simmered against his, her eyelids fluttering shut, the arousal simmering in the pit of her belly flaring demandingly.

"So…we just have to amuse ourselves for the foreseeable future?" she asked, with laughter in her voice when she felt his fingers moving over her nipples. "Is that what you are trying to tell us?"

Adrian's concerned look had evaporated.

"You're a cheeky sort," Seth commented.

Lily rolled onto her back between them. She was turned on, but she also wanted to know what made him tick. "I'm also sharper than you give me credit for." She gave him a knowing look. "You are using sex to distract us."

"No." He looked down at her with curiosity. "Well...maybe a bit, but the fact you are here made this pretty unavoidable." He shot her an accusing look. "You are trouble, and I knew that the moment I saw you."

"Oh that's right, blame me." Peering up at him, she took a moment to consider the implications of what he'd said, and they were varied. "You don't seduce every couple you have in witness protection?"

His face was a picture. He stared across at Adrian dubiously. "I didn't seduce Adrian."

"Ah, so you admit you seduced me."

He frowned at her, and then rubbed his hand around the back of his neck before answering. It was fascinating for Lily, because he was experiencing the same sort of dilemmas she was, the morning after the day before. Last night it had been so simple. Now she was confused. Seth, too, was clearly uneasy with the idea that she thought he'd seduced another man, not to mention the fact he'd moved in on Adrian's date.

She tapped his chest with one finger. "Just trying to get a rise out of you."

His mouth tightened in a wry smile, and then he nodded at Adrian. "You're with Adrian. I don't do relationships."

They both stared at him. Lily hadn't realised he was thinking along those lines as well.

"Seriously," Adrian commented, with mock surprise. "You've never shagged a woman before?"

"Now you're just pushing your luck that bit too far." Seth shook his head. "I'm just an add-on feature here, is what I mean."

"An add-on?" This was a bit of a dilemma for him, Lily realised, even as she teased him about it. He shouldn't be in bed with either of them, she supposed. "Like a sex toy, huh? Comes with a screw-in attachment that will have you moaning with pleasure."

Seth lifted one eyebrow at her, but the comment had diffused his tension. "So, have you ever done this kind of thing before?" he asked, his thigh resting heavily against hers again.

He was good at changing the subject, Lily noted. "What, get stranded in Wales in police custody?" She stuck her tongue out at him, but she loved how this felt, the simmering arousal, the playful banter. It echoed the hot, easy-going intimacy she had felt with Adrian online. Something tickled the back of her consciousness all the same. The joke she had made in passing about Seth doing this to distract them. Was he? All of it, even the easy going attitude? Had he picked that up from Adrian? Was he the sort of man you could ever get close to, really? She pushed the thought away, because she didn't like the way it felt.

Seth nudged the duvet down, making it obvious he was taking a better look at her. "You know what I mean, taking on two men at the same time."

"No. I've never done this before. In fact," she said, thinking aloud, "I never even thought about anything like this, and I've had some pretty wild fantasies." Her face heated, because the way they were both staring at her made her wish she hadn't said that. "Shut up," she declared.

Seth shrugged. "We didn't say a word."

He might not have said a word, but his cock was getting harder.

"You were thinking something though, weren't you?"

"Nothing at all." He nudged his erection against her hip. "Right now, my brain is completely empty. I have no clue why."

Adrian laughed.

Moaning softly, she wriggled between them. Turning to face Adrian, she found his cock solid against her belly. Automatically, her hand closed around it.

Seth grumbled at her back, his cock upright and hard in the groove where her thighs met. Resting a kiss against her shoulder, he breathed her in then growled, before biting her playfully. There he was on that sensitive spot again. It was like he knew exactly what it did to her. "I do hope this isn't a cold shoulder."

"Luckily for you, it isn't." She opened her legs and trapped his rock-hard cock between her thighs, squeezing it hard. He groaned, and she purred, her hands closing over Adrian's upright cock. Adrian kissed her, his hands cupping her face, his cock pushing gratefully into her hands. Seth kissed and bit into her shoulder from behind while his cock slid in and out between her thighs, the slick head moving against her sensitive inner thighs, making her clit throb.

Seth's hand reached around to rest on her pussy. Against her back she felt how hard his muscles were, the wall of his chest and the tight ridges of his abdomen. Rolling her hips, she moaned into Adrian's mouth as he kissed her. Seth's fingers rubbed her clit in a self-assured, almost lazy rhythm. "So wet, you naughty lady."

"I wonder why," she responded, breathily, his touch making her clit thrum. Wrapped in them both, the double-dose of machismo that surrounded her made her feel lush, rich to overflowing with female power. She was so wet her thighs were slick, and his fingers slid readily between her folds, sending waves of pure ecstasy deep inside her. Bound up in the unfolding sexual rapport, her body undulated between them.

Glancing down, she marvelled at Adrian's upright cock in her hands, the way it bowed, the swollen crown, the slick opening. Running her thumb against its sensitive underside, she gasped as he tweaked her nipple in return. Her thighs tightened on Seth's cock.

"Oh yes, like that, squeeze tight," Seth encouraged, thrusting faster, his fingers homing in on her clit, rolling back and forth over it.

She was totally given over to the decadent experience of hands and cocks and fingers and sticky wet pleasure, her climax on the horizon. Adrian's eyes closed, then opened, and his gaze seared her, so intense that she felt his need as though it were inside her.

I want him; I want to feel him inside me while he looks at me like that.

It was too late to change their position. The symbioses of their three bodies in motion was so intoxicating that she lost herself in the moment, her orgasm blossoming, the grind of hips and hands in mutual masturbation fated to fulfil.

Adrian arched his head back, the muscles in his neck cording, his face contorting as his cock jerked in her hands. She buckled when she felt his hot semen on her skin, her body tightening, her spine rigid, before she melted into relinquishment. As she did, Seth thrust hard and fast, and she heard his grunt of release close behind her, his mouth resting against her ear as he soaked her thighs and pulled free.

Panting, she moved her hands to her belly then up to her breasts, massaging them there, the slick essence of Adrian's semen like a signature on her, a brand she wanted to wear, proudly. Her thighs were stained with Seth, her breasts and hands with Adrian.

"Bloody hell." Adrian stared at her.

"I don't want to forget," she whispered, trying to explain her strange, instinctive ritual.

"I don't think any of us will forget this." Seth's lips brushed over her neck and her skin was so sensitive she moaned aloud.

"No. Let's just enjoy it, life's short." It was Adrian.

Looking into his eyes, she saw all the things that he had tried to hide from her. The deep concerns; the need to know that he was doing the right thing. She saw and felt it all, and she knew what else he was thinking—that she wouldn't have slept with him if it hadn't been for Seth. That was wrong, so wrong. Reaching out, she found his hand and meshed her fingers with his

Deep inside her she wanted to hold the moment forever, to hold both of them and chase away the world. Instead, a face flashed in her mind—the face of the man who had been in the elevator with her in London. Doubts crowded in, like unwelcome shadows, shadows that Lily resented. Mustering all her inner strength, she pushed them away. Pure pleasure was at their fingertips, and who knew what lay beyond—tomorrow, or the day after that. Her friend Andrea was always telling her to live for the moment. For the first time ever, Lily totally understood the sentiment. "We're here together, let's enjoy every minute. It would be wrong not to grab the chance for happiness when it happens like this."

"You're not wrong there," Seth said, and Adrian nodded, gratefully, putting the seal on it for her.

Chapter Ten

Emery Lavonne stood in the entrance of the East End grill bar Keane had designated as a meeting venue and grimaced. The place was noisy and reeked of fast food and high cholesterol. A waitress was on her way over, but he spied Jason Keane sitting in a booth nearby and headed over. He recognised him from his photos on police records, always a sign of criminal pedigree. Keane was tucking into a burger, and he didn't stop eating when Lavonne joined him.

Sliding into the seat opposite, Lavonne noticed a lone man sitting on the other side of the restaurant, watching. A bodyguard? Jason Keane would have at least two minders, much like Carlisle. Between them they were responsible for a large percentage of London's drug trafficking, and they always travelled in packs.

"Coffee, black," Lavonne said, when the waitress appeared. "That's all."

Keane wiped his mouth with his paper napkin and eyed Lavonne across the table, then he took an envelope out of his pocket and put it on the table between them. "How long will this take? Mr Carlisle is understandably eager to have his errant accountant taken care of as quickly as possible."

"There's been a change of location." He shrugged. "High profile witness, it happens."

"And?" Keane narrowed his eyes.

"And the sooner I'm done here," he said, pointedly, "the sooner I can find out where that is."

Keane picked at his teeth for a moment, annoyance flickering in his eyes. "So why did you offer to do this, don't the police pay you enough?"

"Think what you like." He'd got a taste for the killing. That wasn't something you admitted to, especially when you were a policeman. Eighteen months before he'd killed for the first time, whilst protecting a witness. The buzz was unlike anything else he'd ever experienced, and he'd craved more of it. He'd fought it, for a while. Then he didn't fight anymore. Now he had to deal with Seth Jones and the job promised to be doubly rewarding. He'd never liked Jones. He'd have his man soon enough.

The waitress arrived with his coffee. He took a mouthful and then pushed the cup away. "Was there something else?"

Keane looked across the table with undisguised animosity. "I don't have any faith in you. I want you to know that I'm only going along with this because Eric does, and I have to respect that. I have, however, told him I have my doubts. If you mess up, you'll make my day."

Lavonne faked a smile. "If you're trying to motivate me, it's really not necessary."

"We'll see."

He stood up, pocketed the envelope of money, and left. Glancing back over his shoulder, he noticed Keane nod at his henchman. They were going to try to follow him. Lavonne smiled to himself. If they thought they were going to use him to find Walsh they had another thing coming.

Not going to happen, buddy. This is my kill.

* * * *

Adrian and Seth were in the kitchen hunting for food, when Adrian spotted the clock on the cooker and noticed it was near one in the afternoon. He was starting to lose all sense of time, as well as all sense of the outside world. Was that a good thing, or a bad thing, he wondered?

"We're almost out of milk." Seth grabbed a box of cereal and dipped into it, eating it directly from the box. "I'll have a cup of tea and then go get some fresh supplies."

Adrian plugged the kettle in and then leaned against the work surface. "Is it far?"

Seth shook his head. "I'll be gone forty minutes, maybe less." He had that assessing look in his eyes. "Can I trust you two to stay inside and out of view?"

"Yes, of course." He was trying to picture where they were in Wales. He'd visited Cardiff, but he didn't know this area at all. How far away was the nearest town?

Seth lifted three cups out of a cupboard and opened the tea caddy. He glanced back at Adrian while he did so. "Should I be apologising to you, about Lily?"

Adrian was surprised, and amused. He resisted the urge to chuckle, and stared at Seth, deadpan. Shrugging, he waited expectantly. After a moment, Seth put the tea caddy down and raised his hands, a tea bag rather comically clutched between the fingers of one hand. "Look mate, I'm sorry, it just sort of happened."

Adrian laughed. "I'm kidding…although I have to say it is good of you to apologise." He smiled. Seth relaxed, visibly. He really had been worried. "It's not the sort of thing that anyone can orchestrate," he added. "It just happened. As you said, it took all three of us to agree to it. Lily was up for it, I enjoyed it, and if it hadn't been for your presence it might never have happened."

"It would have happened," Seth responded. "She was ready for you when she arrived at your office." He shook his head. "Man, was she ever ready."

Adrian paused before replying to that one. "I'm not going to lie, I do wish I had been the one who opened the door, but things might have taken a very different turn. As my secretary is always telling me, we have to believe in fate sometimes, especially when it deals us out such a bloody good hand as this one."

"Agreed." There was respect in Seth's eyes.

"I'd be climbing the walls here if it wasn't for Lily, what with the case pending."

Seth nodded.

The black clouds on his horizon crowded in again. "I don't want to regret agreeing to give evidence, but I have to say, it's doing my head in right now."

"It's natural. Think about how you'd feel if you hadn't come forward. You'd still be at his beck and call, and that would only escalate once he got a hold on you."

"That's true."

Seth had been with witnesses before, many times. This kind of stress would be something he'd be familiar with.

"Thanks."

"Any time, really. If you want to talk, I'm here."

"There is something I'm curious about. Why did you change the location? Not that I'm complaining, mind you. This place is great, very comfortable. I'm just curious."

"The attempt," Seth answered, simply, eyes downcast. "Just wanted to be doubly sure."

Silence hung between them for a moment, and then Adrian reached out and put his hand on Seth's shoulder. "I appreciate everything you've done for my safety, mine and Lily's."

Seth gave a lopsided smile. "It's my job."

Lily wandered in. She was wearing one of the T-shirts Seth had offered, socks, and not a lot else. As she joined them she looked the pair of them over, a bemused smile took up residence on her face. "I'm not interrupting a special moment between you two, am I?"

Seth frowned. "Huh?"

"You two seemed to be getting so much closer...should I be jealous?" Her eyes rounded and then she winked. "I mean, you will still need me at bedtime, right?"

"No way, you can't be serious." Seth laughed. "I don't mind sharing, but it's this I'm after." He spanked her firmly on the bottom, and Lily jolted and then moaned, audibly, eyelids lowering.

"Whereas me, on the other hand..." Adrian said, adopting a deadpan expression again. He waited until they both looked his way. Lily looked fascinated, Seth wary. "I've always wondered what it would feel like, to make another man come."

Seth looked seriously disturbed, and then Adrian laughed.

Seth reached again for the cereal packet, shaking his head. "You've got a seriously warped sense of humour. You're ganging up on me, the pair of you."

The clouds had gone again, at least for the time being, and Adrian preferred it that way.

* * * *

The shower cubicle in Adrian's en-suite bathroom was large, which was just as well. Lily stood just outside of the fall of water with her back against the tiled wall. Steam filled the cubicle—steam, and the sound of her sighs of approval.

Adrian was facing her, the spray from the shower beating against his back. With his palms alternately cupped and splayed, he soaped her breasts—slowly, luxuriously—and he'd been doing it for at least a minute. Lily was in heaven.

Seth had gone to get milk and bread and once he'd left them, Adrian led her to the shower. First he'd shampooed her hair, carefully, silently. Lily was still in a haze of pleasure from what had gone before, and she felt languid and cherished as he washed her. With intricate care, he'd soaped her hands and arms, his cock half-risen as he did so. His hair was plastered to his head, and it made him look even leaner, the line of his jaw constantly drawing her hand to it. He stared at her as if learning every inch of her body, and now his attention to her breasts had turned into an erotic massage of which she had never known the like. Watchful and responsive to her sighs, he had sensitised her breasts to the extreme, kneading them gently and then tweaking the nut hard nipples, alternating between the two. Lily sighed with ecstasy.

"When I first said I'd give evidence, I never imagined I would be doing something like this while in witness protection."

She rested her hands on his shoulder for balance, looking deep into his eyes. "No, I never even thought that we'd be able to get this intimate on our first date, let alone spend so much time together."

He nodded happily. "I didn't dare think about it beyond the first meeting. I just wanted that to go well, hoping that we could experience a bit of what we'd had online."

"This is even better." She nodded down at where his hands were squeezing her. "That's so, so good," she added, breathlessly. "I actually think you could make me come like that."

"You reckon?" Holding his gaze with hers, he stroked her breasts for a moment longer, and then kissed her, long and slow, before continuing. "That's good to know, but I really want to be inside you when you come."

Lily's pussy fluttered with expectation, and then he bent down to take one nipple in his mouth, his hands cupping both breasts as he did so.

"Are you sure your dodgy knee is up to it?" She managed to get the words out while she clenched her hands to stay focused. Her nipples were so hard they stung and the one he was licking burned as he sucked on it and then grazed it with his teeth, sending a jagged riff from her breasts to her centre and back again. Her clit pounded, and she blinked into the steam as she rested her head back against the tiled wall, barely able to stand.

"It's fine, and I'm more than ready." Adrian lifted his head and moved his hand, stroking his entire palm up and down the mound of her pussy, kneading it as he did so.

"Believe me, I am so ready. All those weeks of foreplay, the anticipation." He shook his head. "Watching you with Seth is such a turn on. The only thing that has stopped me going completely insane last night and this morning is the fact that you are so damn good with your mouth and your hands." His fingers made their way inside her, and she could see he was barely holding back as he thrust one finger into her sex, his erection long and hard against her hip. "But now I need to fuck you, badly."

Lily moaned.

"I want to be inside you when you come," he repeated.

"In that case you better get us back to the bed, quickly." She gasped when he thrust another finger inside her. "Especially if you are going to continue doing that."

His eyes seemed to light, and his grin was wicked. With one hand claiming her pussy, he plucked her nipple with the other, pulling on it until she cursed, loudly.

She reached for the shower faucet, and turned it off. "I'm not kidding! On the bed, quickly."

Adrian laughed when she staggered out of the cubicle, grabbing his hand as she went. He lifted a towel as they passed the rail, but when he went to dry her off she flung herself on the bed on her back.

"Hurry," she said.

But Adrian paused and he nodded down at her groin. "Show me."

He was standing at the edge of the bed, her viewpoint placing him right between her thighs, right where he'd told her he'd stand in all those raunchy chats they'd shared. Moaning, she lifted her feet, planting them on the bed, opening her legs as she did so, baring her pussy to him.

"Touch yourself; I want to see it, long to see it." His cock was rigid and tapping against his belly. He stroked himself, one hand riding up and down, rhythmic and purposeful on his cock.

With her fingers, she splayed her pussy, moving over its slick surface. Her folds were engorged and hot, and her clit beat wildly, so swollen and expectant that when she touched it her back arched against the bed. "Please, Adrian."

"Please what?"

"Please. I want you, now."

"Ah, ah, ah," he teased, wagging a finger at her, eyes warm and filled with desire and affection. "I *am* going to fuck you, believe me. But I'm living the dream, lady, all the things you put in my head. I'm living out the promise. Make yourself come, I want to see it. Then you'll get the rest."

Knees lifted, urgency swamping her, she rubbed herself quickly for relief. It didn't take long, not in her current state. With her clit captured between two fingers, she squeezed it then rolled back and forth until she climaxed, her body feverish because of the way he was watching her, so obviously wanting her and ready to go.

He strode to the bedside cabinet, where Seth had left a box of condoms, and quickly pulled one out and on. Then he was there, between her legs, his sheathed cock pressed upright between the lips of her pussy.

Lily's head thrashed against the pillows, her hips lifting against the rigid shaft, her clit thrumming with sensation. "I want you, want you so badly."

"Music to my ears, lover." He manoeuvred his cock to her opening and drove inside in one swift, possessive movement.

It took her breath away, making her spine stretch. Her thighs locked around his hips, heels against the back of his legs, her body clamping onto him, inside and out.

He threw back his head, neck corded, bellowing unreservedly as he rode her. "Oh, that is so bloody good."

Delighted, Lily met him and matched him. Her lips parted each time he thrust inside her, her breath caught on each move. He locked eyes with her, nodding. With her hands on his upper arms, she looked deep into his eyes, loving the way he was.

"Long time coming, love," he said, stroking her damp hair back across the pillows. "This has been a long time coming."

It surely had been, and they were frantic in their union, their hips rising together in time, each of them urging the other on. "Faster," she said, embracing his cock over and over, joyous laughter escaping her lips, "harder."

There was such a look of pride in his eyes that her chest ached. "Oh, Adrian…"

"Right here, love, I'm right here." His voice wrapped around her like an embrace, taking her to the edge. With her arms and legs locked tight around him, she came, her body pulsating with heat and energy.

Grinding deep, his cock jerked and then he stilled, silent in his moment of release. Holding the position for as long as he could, he kissed the tip of her nose, before rolling away onto the bed next to her. His fingers meshed with hers, and he took her hand to his lips, kissing it.

She had all but melted into the bed, her limbs like jelly, and she was about to comment on that fact, when he got up and went into the bathroom and was back a minute later, reaching for another condom.

"Blimey," she said, rising up onto her elbows to observe, "you're still hard."

"Like I said, I've been waiting, and I developed a whole head of steam these past weeks." He grinned. "Now I've started, I could work my way through this whole box of condoms."

"You really can go again, straight away?" Lily was astonished.

"Uhuh, I can usually manage twice, sometimes three rounds." The new condom was on. "Can you take more?"

Laughing huskily, she reached out to him. She had two men, and apparently one of them could go all night. It never rained but it poured. "I think so, but I may never walk again."

That was when the door creaked open.

"I can't turn my back for a moment," Seth said, taking off the baseball cap he was wearing and throwing it onto the bed next to them. "You're insatiable."

"Hey, it's my turn now," Adrian murmured, resuming his former position and thrusting hard between Lily's thighs again.

Lily savoured the look Seth was giving her, a thorough once up-and-down with an appreciative grin.

"Are you going to join us?" she asked.

"Hell no, I thought I might try this watching thing, see what all the fuss is about." He waved his hand. "Carry on." Humour filled his eyes, and Lily laughed softly, mellow and wildly aroused all at once, drugged by the experience.

This time Adrian was less hurried, and his slow, almost lazy thrusts made her melt all over again. When he bent his head to kiss her throat, she saw how Seth had changed, how his expression had darkened to brooding. Glancing lower, she saw he was hard inside his jeans.

He moved closer, watching.

She growled, clutching at Adrian, decadent in her excess, eyes closing as another orgasm rolled over her. Adrian's mouth was on her neck, and when Seth's mouth closed over hers, the pair of them kissing her as she peaked, she was in heaven, and she wanted it to last and last.

Chapter Eleven

"Day four in the Big Brother witness protection house," Adrian said, faking a reality show voiceover, "and the lovely *Laidbacklady* Lily grows more ravishing by the moment, keeping both Seth and Adrian in a constant state of arousal."

He munched on a piece of toast, watching as Lily rolled on the sofa, giggling. The way her eyes sparkled made him feel good. Even Seth was smiling. It hadn't slipped his notice that Seth rarely smiled in that genuine way, except when it was about Lily.

"That's great. Can you do other impersonations?" Lily asked.

"Keep the curtains closed and stay away from the windows," he said, mimicking Seth.

Lily laughed again, and Seth's eyebrows shot up.

"You're crazy," Lily said, reaching for her tea.

"In a good way or a bad way?" They kept asking each other that question.

"A good way, of course." She looked cosy on the sofa. She'd pulled a velvet cover over her legs, and clutched her breakfast mug in both hands to warm her. "It is a bit like Big Brother, isn't it? Day three, and the housemates don't know what bloody time of day it is, but they eat breakfast, because they just got up and they were hungry." Flashing a smile his way, she sat quietly for a moment and then sighed, loudly. "It's way different to the normal routine, for me at any rate. What would your average day be like?"

Adrian relished her question. "Well...there's this woman who I like to talk dirty with, online..."

"No!" She laughed again, and looked at him fondly, as if she liked the joke. "I mean the rest, the bits that I don't know about." She really did want to fill the missing pieces of the picture. "What would you be doing now?"

"Right about now," he glanced at his watch, "my secretary, Cassandra, would be breaking the endless cycle of figures with a cup of green tea and a large bowl of muesli."

Seth coughed. "You're a health freak? Damn, I missed that on the info sheet."

They had info sheets? "Me no. I'll pretty much eat anything. Cassandra, yes. She's like this 1970's super-efficient health freak, into yoga and the whole thing. She frets that I don't eat breakfast, and—like I said—I will eat anything that's put in front of me."

"This is the grandmother lady who thinks you should get out and meet women?" A teasing, curious smile lit Lily up again.

"The very one." He paused, remembering the time he had shared that with her, thinking about the times they had shared on line. It also made him think about Cassandra, who he cared about a great deal—thinking about the actual nuts and bolts of what went on when he was pulled out of his life. Looking Seth's way, he knew he had to ask. "Will Cassandra know? I mean, will someone have explained it to her, and my brother. Will they understand what's happened to me?" He wasn't sure he wanted them to know, they'd only worry, but the question kept bugging him.

Seth nodded. "Normally you'd have had time to alert them yourself, but the way things panned out, members of my department would have moved in and checked out the office. Your next of kin and secretary's details were already on file."

"Good. She'd have been worried." Why did he suddenly feel so weighted down by all of this? A moment ago it was good, it was free and easy.

"Yes, my flatmate will be worried too." Lily's expression had also grown more serious. She cast an accusing glance in Seth's direction.

"That's different," he countered, quickly, a heavy frown developing on his forehead.

"Why?" Adrian asked.

"If my department tracks down the bloke Lily saw, she can go home." Seth grew tense, his cheeks working as if he was grinding his teeth. "This will be sorted soon, Lily, I promise, and you'll be able to get back to your regular life."

Silence descended on them. Adrian felt gutted. Ultimately he was in a lose-lose situation. If Lily was gone, this would be so much worse, but he hated that she was here because of him. Confused, and regretting he had asked, he stood up. "I'm going to take a shower."

"Are you okay?" Lily said, concerned. "You already had a shower,"

"I need another." He paused, looked back, and smiled her way. "I'm okay, just need to think."

Limping off down the hallway, he realised that no amount of thinking—or showering—was going to help this particular problem. The one he'd unexpectedly found himself burdened with, the one that was extra to the Carlisle court case and everything that came with that. He didn't want Lily to be here, but he did. Whilst he recognised that she was making the most of a bad lot, she'd never be able to forgive him not afterwards, not after they got back to their real life, and that brought him a whole of pain.

* * * *

Seth knew they were both upset, and he knew it was because they were talking about what they'd left behind. Adrian had to come to terms with it, but Lily didn't. He had to out Lavonne, then she could go.

Simple as that. Except it wasn't.

Looking over at her, he felt as if he'd learnt so much about her in these few days. He'd begun to know what made her tick, and he knew it was taking a lot of inner strength for her not to balk right now, not to shuck off his authority and make life difficult again. He was prepared; sometimes the witnesses needed to let off steam. Better that they attack him for his role in this than walk out and into danger. And she, more than anyone, had the right to attack him. He needed to sort it, needed to find a way to safely have Lavonne arrested so that she could go back to her normal life. No reason not to, right?

Problem was he was thinking about ways to do that less and less as time went by, because he liked having her there. He was honest with himself on that score. Nevertheless, it rested a heavy sense of guilt on his shoulders.

"Tell me about the online chat thing," he said, asking about the grey area in his understanding of her.

"What about it?" She looked as if she thought he might be judging her.

"How did you get into it? I'm just curious." He reached out and teased her tootsies with his.

She foot wrestled him, and then rested her head back on the cushions. "Oh, well it was kind of a joke, at first. I haven't had a proper relationship since I was in training as a nurse. When Andrea, my flatmate, made the decision to open the sandwich boutique, I left nursing, and things only got busier. We're in the first year of a new business."

"That's hard work."

"Yes, in fact these past few days have actually felt like a bit of a holiday for me, one I probably needed." She paused, a frown gathering between her eyebrows. "Anyhow, we have this guy who delivers salad and fruit to the boutique."

"Fruit?"

"Yes, some people like grapes in their brie-and-salad baguette."

He grimaced.

She threw him an amused look. "We need to educate your taste buds."

"When it comes to food, I have simple tastes." *When it comes to women, I seem to be attracted to you, and you are so much more complex than I'd ever have guessed.*

Where did that thought come from?

"People can change."

140

There was a teasing expression on her face and she wore a half smile. What was she thinking? He'd love to know.

"So, this guy Carlo," she continued, "he is recently divorced and he's always going on about meeting these sexy women online. We thought he was joking or that he was using dating agencies, but when we asked him about it, it turned out he was using chat rooms. For him it's too soon to get involved with another woman properly, but he likes to keep his chat-up skills polished just in case — or so he says." She smiled at that point.

Seth wondered if she had a soft spot for Carlo.

"For me it was different reason, very little time, and I was just looking for a bit of fun." She shrugged. "Honestly, it was just a giggle to begin with. In fact, the first time Andrea and I logged in together and pretended we were twins." She laughed, remembering. "We said we were looking for one guy, to share…we got dozens of men wanting to chat with us."

"I can imagine."

"We literally ran away, laughing. It was way over the top. Then I went in on my own one time, and I happened to get chatting with Adrian."

He stared at her, reflecting how lucky Adrian must have felt conversing with her, then meeting her. He also reflected on all the losers and weirdoes she might have met and might still meet, doing that, and it worried him.

"Did you know there's a stack of food in the freezer?" They had sat in a comfortable silence for a minute or so. Didn't she want to talk about it anymore?

"No, I hadn't checked."

"I'm hungry," she explained, "You two are keeping my appetite up. I did a bit of exploring earlier. How does fish and chips sound for tonight?"

"Now you're talking."

"I thought you'd approve."

A secret smile lit her expression, and it was right then that Seth finally admitted to himself that it didn't matter that she was here because of Adrian. That was then, this was now. She wanted him as well. She'd wanted him when she'd come onto him outside Adrian's office, and it hadn't gone away. For all her prickly attitude towards him and the flippant remarks about enjoying the moment, he could read the signals. God knows he'd had enough time in close quarters with people. He learnt to read how they really felt, no matter what words came out of their mouth. Desire was there in her expression, in the things she didn't say and the way she acted, everything about her told her what he needed to know.

I shouldn't care, he told himself. But he couldn't help it.

She rose to her feet and walked to the curtains, peeking out between them. She was looking longingly at the patio and the landscaped garden beyond. It was a look he'd seen many times before, the familiar look of a caged creature, begging to be free. Why did it bother him that she looked so caged? He'd protected witnesses so many times before, and almost every time he'd seen people start to look this way when their confinement became a burden and they wanted to be free, but this time he was thinking about in a different way. He felt her pain, her longing, and it was because they were involved.

It had been an incredibly intense time, the three of them living a fantasy many owned but never fulfilled. Four great days, days he'd never forget, but he shouldn't have done it, because he couldn't help himself, not when it came to Lily. It had to end, soon.

"It looks so beautiful out there this morning. Not as sunny as it was, but the sky is roaring. It's such a beautiful spot. I'd love to explore. Another time, of course."

The fact she liked his childhood home made him smile, he couldn't help it. Then she turned around and the look of yearning on her face made him feel so bloody bad.

Shit. *I could do without this.*

The sense of responsibility he felt towards her, a woman he'd got involved with—the only woman he'd got involved with under these circumstances—was different, definitely. He felt he owed her more, which is why he shouldn't have got involved in the first place. If he started making concessions to security for her, as he was tempted to do, weak points would be opened up. Even so, he nodded. "I could turn the alarms off, if you want to go outside for a few quick breaths of air."

Fool, if a local is walking in the fields beyond the gardens and saw that someone is staying here, when it should be closed up and empty, they'll investigate, or report it to the police, which would open up a line for Lavonne.

Her eyes lit up. "You'd do that?"

Surely they couldn't be that unlucky, to be spotted inside a minute? "Just for one minute, and only if you stay on the patio, close to the house."

She masked her disappointment, but not before he caught it. She wandered over. "I'd really appreciate it, just to breathe that crisp air and get some natural light."

He went to the hall to switch off the alarms at the main box, ad she followed, clinging to his arm as if it was Christmas and he was giving her the best present in the world. While he flicked the alarm switches off, he dealt out the rules. "I need to be able to see you at all times, and I want you to stay close to the doors so that you're not visible to anyone who might be walking on the land beyond the gardens. There's a public footpath there, and occasionally people pass through."

"We are safe here, aren't we?" She stared at the alarm box, as if he'd put the doubt in her mind.

It was no bad thing, but still...he hated to see the worried expression of face. "Yes, very safe, as safe as we can be right now. I just have to remain vigilant. It's my job."

"Thanks Seth, I appreciate this." She stood on her tiptoes and kissed him quickly. It was like a promise. Her kisses always felt like promises.

When they walked back to the patio doors, he paused and stroked her hair back from her face. "I'm sorry it can't be more than a minute."

She nodded. He opened the door and she wandered out.

He stood in the doorway watching as she walked up and down the patio a mere three feet away from where he was in the doorway. She was following his rules. Shielding her eyes, she looked first at the landscape beyond, and then she looked at the border shrubs that ran along the patio. If Gareth, his stepfather, had been here, he'd be out there with her telling her the names of the various plants. He always did that when a guest showed interest. They'd like Lily, his parents. She was warm and vivacious. He rubbed the back of his neck with one hand, wondering at the way his thoughts had wandered. It was Lily; she got him so easily distracted. That was not a good thing.

She wrapped her arms close around herself, and he knew that she was cold. It was pretty obvious that she didn't care. She was dressed so inappropriately for a winter morning, he noticed, with that short skirt and the high heels.

It's because she is dressed for a date, a sexy date in London, with Adrian.

I just got lucky and got in on the act.

He cursed himself under his breath. It just wasn't right, any of it. The most important rules of his job were to always remain vigilant, and never get emotionally involved. What was wrong with him? He was failing to concentrate. Perhaps he was too old for the job. It happened. Whatever it was, the niggling doubts he had faded as he watched Lily. She was coming back to the house.

"My minute is up, thank you." A smile hovered around her mouth. Once he stood back, she stepped outside the door and looked at him. "I need to ask you for something."

That sounded heavy. "Go ahead."

Her cheeks turned pink. "I need some underwear."

He frowned. "Underwear?"

"I only had the one pair of knickers, obviously." She flashed him a glance that showed she really didn't want to have to ask him about this. "I've been washing them and drying them on the radiator overnight, but you tore them, yesterday."

"Right." Staring at her, he felt stupid. He should have thought of it. Normally his witnesses in protection were prepared, at least with an overnight bag. Not this one. With Adrian it was easy; he'd passed on some of his own gear. He hadn't even thought about Lily, except how good she looked in what she was wearing. Then again, when he was thinking about her underwear, he was mostly thinking about taking it off.

He shook his head. Yep, he was well and truly a lost cause over this woman. "Come on, I'm sure we can find you something, upstairs."

Lily cocked her head on one side as she looked up at him, but didn't comment. He locked the patio doors and took her hand, leading her into the hallway.

"Hold on." He walked over to the control panel and flicked the alarms back on. Lily watched, and nodded. She followed him up the staircase, looking around with curiosity. There were several more rooms on the first floor that she hadn't seen before. Seth led her to another staircase, at the top of which was the door he'd checked was locked at the outset. She stared at the 'private' sign on the door. Seth unlocked the door and ushered her in, watching as she walked into the private space.

"Oh, wow, what a fantastic view." She walked across the sitting area to the picture window, which was directly above the patio she'd been on earlier. Gareth, his step dad, plotted and planed all his planting from up here. His aerial view, as he called it.

Seth shut the door and walked in, glancing around. He'd been here just a few weeks before, at Christmas, but he was seeing it through her eyes.

"Oh, my God, this is you." She'd lifted a framed photo from the sideboard.

Shit. He strode over and snatched it out of her hand, but she wrestled him for it, grasping it in both hands and holding it up next his face, chucking as she did so. "What were you, eighteen?"

Seth could have kicked himself, he hadn't thought this through. "Thereabouts."

She looked at it from under her lashes, and that knowing look that women got appeared on her face. "I bet you had lots of female attention. I certainly would've been interested."

Seth reached for the photograph when she was off guard, putting it back in its position on the sideboard.

Her expression grew more serious, and he knew the penny had dropped. "This isn't a safe house at all, is it? This is your family home."

Seth gritted his teeth.

"But that's not your name on the licence by the door. Your name is Jones, isn't it?"

She was good. "My mum remarried."

She looked at him thoughtfully and then her eyes rounded and she stared at him as if horrified. "If this isn't the safe house...and you brought us here." She slowed, truly freaked. "You're not...you're not working for this man, Carlisle, are you?" She didn't exactly back away, but she looked as if she was about to.

Seth grasped her around the shoulders, hating to see the mistrust that had risen in her expression. "No. There was a reason why I couldn't take Adrian to the designated safe house."

"What reason?"

Shit. He'd have to tell her, because she wouldn't feel safe with him. If he didn't tell her she would keep asking and then Adrian would find out. "I'll explain why, if you promise to keep it to yourself. Adrian has got enough on his mind; I don't want to add to his worries. Promise me you won't tell him what I'm about to tell you?"

"Yes, if you feel that's the right thing to do."

Was she starting to accept his authority? He thought she'd just mellowed, but she really was playing along. He was glad of that. "That man you saw in the corridor, the one who took a shot at Adrian."

"Yes?"

"I also saw him, from the fire escape. And I recognised him. He's a fellow officer."

Her eyes rounded. "You mean..."

"My guess is he's on Eric Carlisle's payroll. Once I knew that, I couldn't risk taking Adrian to the safe house. A policeman in the same department as me can access that information on the system. This seemed like the best alternative option. " He glanced around the familiar room. "My parents run this place; it's where I grew up. They have an eight-week break in Spain every year, January and February."

"Right. So why don't you report him to the police, to your guys?"

"It's knowing who to trust."

"I see." She stared at him with a heavy expression. "I understand that, believe me. The reason I left nursing, it was partly to do with a senior member of staff who I didn't think was acting appropriately with a patient's care. I took it into my own hands. It was the right move, but my senior got annoyed and said I couldn't accept authority, that I'd acted without her agreement. The hospital backed her up. I handled it the wrong way, and I left, but deep down I know I did the right thing for the patient."

For several moments, they stared into each other's eyes, acknowledging the common ground. Then he found himself scooping her in against him to hold her. With her hands wrapped around his back, it felt natural, it felt good.

He didn't want to have to tell her, tell either of them, but when he held her in his arms that sense of loneliness that he always nursed evaporated for a few moments. "I need to make contact with my boss, but I'm not going to use a phone or e-mail or anything that can pinpoint a location to anyone in the office."

"It all makes sense now." She looked up at him. "Any other ideas?"

"I'm working on it."

"Can you send your boss an e-mail from an anonymous Hotmail account?"

"IP addresses can be traced." As he said it he noticed his step dad's computer on a small desk in the corner of the room, and an idea started to form. It was the mention of the Hotmail account. He had one that he rarely used. "Wait, hold that thought. You might have something there."

The PC was old, and ran on a slow modem. His step dad only used it to run a simple web site advertising the hotel, and his mother occasionally sent Seth family photos to his Hotmail account. Seth walked over and switched the thing on.

"You've had an idea?" Lily was beside him as he took up the seat at the desk.

"Maybe." He did, but by the time he'd got online and opened his account, doubt had slowed him up. He paused, thinking carefully through the idea. It was dangerous, everything was dangerous, but it was the least dangerous thing he'd thought of so far.

Scrolling through messages, he saw the one he was looking for, a party invitation from Colleen Ward. He opened it. A JPEG filled the screen, an image of a clown holding a bunch of balloons.

"Colleen Ward?" Lily had one hand on his back as she looked over his shoulder at the screen.

Seth briefly thought about sending her away, but she would be so curious that it was likely to cause more problems, because she already knew too much. He hit reply and began to type.

> *Colleen, thank you for inviting me to your birthday party last month. I had a great time, even though I ate too much of your mummy's lovely cake. Please tell your dad that Uncle Seth says next time we have to play whack-a-mole, instead of musical chairs. Hugs and kisses from Uncle Seth*

"Uncle Seth?" she looked amused.

"Yes, she's my chief's daughter, so what?"

She shrugged. "Just learning. Very clever," she added nodding at the screen. "Whack-a-mole." She chuckled. "Do you think it will work? I mean, will she tell him?"

"She's an extremely bright kid, and apparently she checks her email every day. Gets excited about receiving mail, so she will mention it. In fact she will bug him so much we'll have to play the game next time I get to visit." He chuckled.

Lily's hand tightened on his shoulder.

"And, most importantly, her dad will know there's a leak at work, because I've gone via an outside route." He reread the message, thought through the implications, and hit send. Before he could start brooding on his decision, he closed down the computer connection. She was still looking at him with a curious expression on her face and a half smile. "Hopefully our shooter will be behind bars, and soon."

He stood up and slapped her playfully on the bottom. "Let's see if we can find you some underwear."

"Do you have a sister?"

"Unfortunately not," Seth replied as he led her towards his parent's bedroom. Frowning, he wondered what the hell he was doing bringing her up here to his mother's room looking for clothes. *Because I can't have her knickers hanging off driving me insane, that's why.* He gestured into the bedroom and then at the chest of drawers is on the far side. "See if you can find something in there."

Moments later he heard her giggle softly. "I don't think your mum and I are the same size." She turned to face him, holding up a rather large pair of pink knickers.

"This was a bad idea," he mumbled vaguely. Size and colour were not the problem. He'd realised that he had no inclination to see Lily in his mother's underwear. Lily had returned her attention to the drawers, bending down as she did so. Her skirt rode up and he got a flash of her bare bottom.

She wasn't wearing any underwear, torn or not.

His cock immediately hardened at the sight of her pussy and bottom, bent over like that, wiggling. "Forget it," he said. "I'll take you to a shop."

"Are you sure it will be safe," she queried, still bent over the drawers.

Staring at her exposed pussy, Seth shook his head. None of them were safe with her walking around like that. His barriers were dropping all over the place, but he had to get her arse covered up and soon, or he'd lose focus altogether.

Chapter Twelve

When Adrian had brooded and sulked long enough to make him feel ashamed of himself, he emerged from his room and walked into the kitchen, which he found empty. In the hallway, he heard creaking floorboards that sounded as if it was on the stairs above, so he wandered to the residents' lounge. His knee was feeling much stronger, which was a relief, but he didn't want to undo that by tackling the stairs.

In the lounge, the curtains at the window where open a few inches, which was unusual. Curious, he crossed the room and peered out. He looked out at the scene beyond, reflecting on how his world had shrunk from everything that it once was, to what was inside these walls. Just a few days before, he couldn't even stand the thought of going into witness protection, being locked up and away from everything that he knew, and at times it now seemed as if the whole world had vanished off the face the earth and there was only three of them left. Three of them here in this isolated the old manor house with its quaint well-stocked bar, and its creaky floorboards.

Shoving his hands into the pockets of the rather baggy jeans that Seth had given him to wear, he wondered vaguely who they belonged to. He'd asked Seth if they were his, and he'd said something non-committal about finding them somewhere in the house. That seemed like a good enough answer, given the circumstances.

It was uncanny, the way he'd adapted to this strange life inside a couple of days. He was in a strange house in place he didn't know, wearing another man's clothing, and yet he was okay with it. It was Lily who'd made that happen, she'd made this time positive — exceptional, even. He had no doubt it would have been a completely different story had she not been forced to join them. It was quite possible that he was simply burying his head in the sand about Carlisle and the trial — not to mention the fact that someone with a gun would rather he was dead and buried.

Which came first, the attachment to Lily, or the need to escape the oncoming trial? The trial was something he hadn't allowed himself to dwell on too much, he knew that, but a voice in his head kept shouting that it was Lily; it was because she'd proved to be everything he wanted and more. Second-guessing himself meant doubts were being thrown up all the time. He was still kicking himself about taking on the Carlisle account at all, and that messed with his head.

When he heard Lily's voice and her laughter approaching outside the room, he turned away from the window and watched as she darted into the lounge. She threw a pink woollen item on to the sofa.

"Seth found me a couple of sweaters and he has kindly offered to do the honourable thing," she rolled her eyes as she said that, "and take me to the shop to buy some necessities."

Seth was taking her out of here? Why did that make him feel so unsettled? "Necessities?"

She turned around and lifted the back of her skirt, exposing one naked buttock. Adrian was reminded of a poster he had on his wall as a teenager. It had a tennis player in exactly the same pose. He shook his head and laughed softly. Her cheeky pose made him want to hold her in his arms. Making his way to a nearby armchair, he grabbed her from behind as he did so, pulling her onto his lap.

"Hey, be careful, watch that leg of yours." Her cheeky expression turned serious.

"Yes, nurse." He rolled her close against him and moved one hand under her skirt to caress the bare buttock she had shown him.

"Ah, I see you're recovering your physical abilities, Mr. Walsh." Her expression softened to a smile again. She put one arm around his back, settling in.

"That I am, so you better beware." He was about to say more when Seth entered the room carrying a scarf in one hand. "Here, you can use this to cover your hair. We have to be quick and discreet about this. It's totally unorthodox, but I guess it has to be done." Glancing in Adrian's direction he added, "Are you okay with this? It won't take much longer than an hour." He looked towards the patio doors. "I'd be much happier if we kept those curtains closed."

Crossing the room, he switched on an up-lighter and a lamp, and then drew the curtains closed.

Adrian noticed that Lily was sparkling. Was she happy, or was she happy to be getting out of here for a while? With Seth. He tightened his grip on her. "We can't have the lady in need of underwear."

She wriggled on his lap. He was getting hard. "So long as you promise you're not going to run-off and leave me here," he added

"Don't be daft." She prodded him in the chest. "It's only 'cos I need undies."

"Yeah, that's what you say now," he teased, "while you are under the influence of Stockholm syndrome."

"Stockholm syndrome?" She looked at him with curiosity. "What's that?"

Adrian immediately wished he hadn't said it. He looked up at Seth, who gave him a concerned glance. "I'm just teasing you, it's nothing."

"No, tell me what it is. I want to know." She wasn't going to let him get away with it. She chuckled, as if she thought it must be some sort of joke, which was his original intention, badly timed though it was.

It was Seth who answered. "It's a term that refers to a state of sympathetic and emotional attachment, specifically where captives get involved with the person who is their captor." His voice was gruff and although he spoke knowledgeably, it clearly made him uncomfortable to do so. "It's traditionally used to talk about kidnappers and their victims," he added, hastily.

"Oh." Her smile faded.

"It was just a joke," Adrian whispered, but she didn't respond.

Stockholm syndrome. He mentally kicked himself for saying it. What was he thinking?

After a moment she turned and hid her face close against his neck, the arm she had draping around his shoulder tightening as she buried her face against him, clinging close. "Don't say that, and don't even think it. That makes it sound as if this is wrong, or...as if it's not real. "

Her response shocked Adrian, and his arms instinctively closed around her upper body, holding her close and stroking her gently. "Hey now, I only meant it as a joke, really, please don't get upset, love."

When he said that she clung to him even tighter, as if to deny it.

He looked across the room at Seth, and shrugged his free shoulder. Seth nodded, indicating he was concerned too. He hung back though, and Adrian knew that this was his problem. He also remembered what Seth said about being an add-on, and that Lily was with him. Did Seth really believe that? Nobody in their right mind would deny the strength of the attraction between Lily and Seth. The situation felt suddenly serious, because it went way beyond his mistimed joke.

Lily sighed against his neck, snuggled closer, still seeking comfort. He didn't want her to be upset—she was usually so strong, bouncing back from everything that happened to her so unexpectedly of the last few days. And yet it also made him see that she didn't want to think this was temporal any more than he did, she didn't want to think their connection was anything to do with being locked up here, away from their normal lives.

That meant she cared.

Something that felt like joy — but was even bigger than that — took hold of him. He stroked her hair and kissed her forehead. "Hey, *Laidbacklady*, this is real. Don't fret."

Eventually she pulled back and looked at him with searching eyes, her pretty mouth down-turned at the corners. God, she was beautiful. The misgiving in her expression only emphasised the open quality she had, that thing he loved about her.

"This time we have together is special, very special, and it's also very real." He moved his hand to her bottom again and waggled his eyebrows. "Would you like me to pinch you to prove it?"

He teased her skin with a gentle pinch. Her expression broke. She laughed and wriggled out of his lap. He let her go, reluctantly, and but held onto one hand, tethering her. When she glanced back, smiling his way, he felt an immense sense of relief. "Are you sure you're okay?"

She didn't pull her hand free, and she nodded. "I'm sorry, that was a bit silly of me, reacting that way."

"No, it wasn't." He squeezed her hand before letting it go. "Enjoy your shopping trip. Take pity on me and buy something black and lacy to wear, I want to see you in something black and lacy."

Chapter Thirteen

Stephen Ward was smiling. Emery Lavonne hadn't seen the chief smiling for some time. He watched as Ward emerged from his glass cubicle with a woman in tow. Curious as to whether it had anything to do with the Adrian Walsh case he made his way to the office gossip's desk. "What's going on?"

Janine looked up from her monitor and beamed, evidently glad of chance to spill. Who needed a newsletter with this woman around? Janine was on the case like a dog with a bone. "Well, it looks as if we might have found out who the mystery woman was; the one Seth Jones took along with his witness when he did a runner."

Lavonne's attention was back with the woman and he memorised her face in case she was an important lead.

"Apparently she reported her flatmate missing at her local station, but they didn't go beyond normal procedures until she called back and mentioned her flatmate had a date. The flatmate had left a note with the name and location. Turns out her date was with Adrian Walsh."

"I see." He cast his mind back. The brunette in the elevator? Could be. She'd been looking at doorways in the corridor when he'd last seen her. He hadn't got a look at the woman's face when Jones was helping her into the car, but it could be the same person.

Janine kept talking, but Lavonne was watching Ward shake hands with the woman. Did this mean that she might have information about where her flatmate was currently located? Ward signalled to a nearby officer to show the woman out of the building. When he returned to his office, he left the door open.

"Looks as if she got more than she bargained for when she went on her date." Janine's voice just about reached him, but Lavonne was already on his way to Stephen Ward's office.

"Morning, Chief, any news on Seth Jones?"

Ward shook his head. "He's still AWOL with the witness, that's assuming they haven't both been taken down…worse case scenario, but we can't rule it out."

Ward was developing a twitch in his cheek. This was really getting to him. It was because it was his buddy who was letting the side down. Reporting that bit of information to the higher authorities must be so hard.

Ward looked up and focused on Lavonne. "Where would you take a witness if there was some reason why you didn't want to use the designated safe house?"

Lavonne shrugged. It was a good question. "Somewhere I could lock down. Somewhere I knew well." His mind was ticking. "Where is home, for Seth Jones?"

Ward took his seat. "Seth's lived in London for the last twelve years or so. He's from Wales, originally." The phone rang. He put up his hand indicating he'd have to take the call. "Stephen Ward." He listened for a moment, frowning. "Look, love, I'm up to my eyeballs in the proverbial here. Tell Colleen I'll talk to her tonight."

Lavonne's attention swept over the papers on the desk while Ward was busy. If he could get his hands on Seth Jones's personal file from human resources, he could perhaps track down the next of kin. Might be a wild goose chase, but he was willing to try anything right now. If he had to deal with Keane phoning him every hour for one more day, he'd get even more trigger happy than he currently was, and it would be Keane who'd be his target. Seth Jones' next of kin was worth a try, and he could sweet talk it from one of the women in HR. His attention moved back to Stephen Ward.

Ward had his fingers pressed against his forehead, but he was surveying the scene outside the glass frontage to his office as the voice on the other end of the phone talked on. After a moment his gaze settled on Lavonne, and he made a move to end the call. "No, you definitely did the right thing. It explains a lot. Give Colleen a hug and tell her we'll definitely play that game."

Family business. Lavonne was itching to get out of the office now that human resources had opened up as a possible avenue of information. He got ready to give his excuses and leave, but when Ward put his phone down he also rose quickly to his feet.

"I appreciate you trying to help out here, but I'm going to have to make a move. I've got a meeting upstairs." He gave a brief, artificial smile, his eyes hooded and thoughtful. "They want to keep tabs on what's happening with this."

Lavonne nodded and left. He headed off in the direction of human resources, but glanced back just as he was about to leave the division. Stephen Ward was still in his office, standing close to the glass frontage, arms folded across his chest. A serious expression shadowed his face as he contemplated the people working outside. For a split-second, their eyes met across the expanse of the witness protection division.

Ward seemed to scrutinise him. Lavonne turned away, shrugging it off. He had a new lead, that's all that mattered. The sooner he took the witness and Jones out of action, the better.

* * * *

Routine, regular solid routine. Focus on the job. Seth repeated the mantra to himself as they sped through the countryside towards Conwy, the nearest town. At the same time he was trying to ignore the woman who sat by his side, peering out at the passing scenery.

"Are you warm enough?" He flicked the heating up a notch.

She nodded and smiled. She was wearing one of his mother's sweaters under her coat. He could handle that. That wasn't underwear. Concentrating on the road, he told himself he couldn't afford to be distracted by her any more. He was a well-respected witness protection officer, and that's because he'd never done anything stupid. Until now. Now his routine had gone to hell because he'd broken his own rules and got involved.

To add to his torment, he wasn't altogether sure he'd done the right thing sending that email message to Ward's daughter. And he'd told Lily about Lavonne. There hadn't been any way out of it at the time, but now he regretted it. He'd even wanted to comfort her over the Stockholm syndrome incident back at the house. How ludicrous was that? The working foundations that had been so solid for him were crumbling. He needed to rebuild them.

A moment later he caught sight of her crossing her legs from the corner of his eye, high on the thigh, making her coat fall open. Still looking out at the scenery, she felt for the coat flap and re-covered her leg with it.

His hands tightened on the steering wheel,

"It's clouding over," she commented. "I think we've seen the last of the winter sun for the time being."

"We've been lucky." He wasn't just talking about the weather.

A few minutes later they were on the bridge that crossed the Conwy estuary and led into the fortress town.

Lily commented on how pretty it was.

"Let's do this, and quickly," he said, as he parked the Land Rover in a car park nestled between the ancient castle and the centre of the small town. It wasn't a big place, but he was pretty sure there was a shop that sold women's stuff of the underwear type. When he switched off the engine, he looked at her. She was hesitant to get out of the vehicle, but wide-eyed, looking around the scenery. "Come on, put the scarf on."

She did as instructed, wrapping the length of fabric around her hair and neck, letting the loose corners dangle down the back of her coat. Satisfied, he walked around to her side of the vehicle and opened the door, watching as she climbed out and gazed up at the castle, entranced. He'd grown up here and it was a familiar landscape, but her enthusiasm for it made him look anew. That's what she was doing to him, breaking him out of familiar patterns. It would be easy to forget the job for a while, with her around. He took her arm and led her quickly away from the car park and across the street towards the shops. They had to get what she needed and get back to the house, sharpish.

They walked quickly through the main thoroughfare. Lily walked quietly and quickly alongside him, her hand inside his.

"Gillian?" A voice queried behind them.

Seth stopped dead, the hairs on the back of his neck standing up. He had a bad feeling about this. Gillian was his mother's name. Glancing back over his shoulder, he saw Annie Conroy, an old friend of his mother's. She was staring at the back of Lily's head with a confused expression. Surely to god she couldn't have recognised his mother's scarf on another woman? A baseball cap and shades was all he needed to go shop for food, but apparently the scarf was a mistake.

Mrs Conroy peered his way, and her eyes lit. "Seth, is that you?"

This was bad news, really bad. Lily had paused and turned around. Mrs Conroy frowned, and looked from one of them to the other.

Damage limitation was the only option. Seth rolled into action. "Mrs Conroy, how lovely to see you." He forced a smile—hopefully a winning one.

The woman's expression melted into a smile. Good sign.

"Seth, it is you. I wondered." She examined Lily again. "Is this your young lady?"

My what? Could this get any more difficult?

Lily gave the older woman a tentative smile, before looking at him expectantly. This sort of complication was just what he had been trying to avoid. He couldn't find a single thing to say. Lily put out her hand to the other woman. "I'm Lily Howard, its lovely to meet someone who knows Seth. He's just been showing me his old haunts."

Fuck it. She'd used her real name. This woman was nothing but a damn liability. He wanted to lock her up and throw away the key. *Should have briefed her, should have been ready.* Seth forced a smile, it took a huge effort. "We were just passing through the area and I decided I'd show her the place I grew up."

Mrs Conroy beamed when Lily put out her hand and rattled a long introduction. "It's a pleasure my dear. I've known Seth since he was born and he attended my Sunday school classes as a wee lad in shorts. It's good to see him with a companion. You must be very special; it's the first time he's brought a young lady home. What a shame his parents aren't at home to meet you."

"It is indeed," Lily responded.

This amused her, for Christ's sake. Seth gritted his teeth. He knew he had to let this run a moment longer or Mrs Conroy's suspicion might bring her up to the house. He was eager to move on and get this outing done with before anyone else who knew him popped up to complicate matters. Her voice droned on, and he disengaged as he scanned the street, reassuring himself but there was no way Lavonne would find them here. They were as undercover as they could get, but it was second nature for him to expect the worse and be ready for it.

"You know, Seth's mother has a scarf just like that. I know because I gave it to her for her birthday, three years ago. "

Bad luck choice, Seth reflected, glaring at the scarf. Nothing got past this woman. She should work for the police. His sense of unease quickly magnified, making his patience evaporate and his temper turn sour. Images of Adrian alone at the house, while they played social butterflies, assailed him. The pavements were getting busier too, as it closed on lunchtime. All of it seemed to mock him and the idiot choices he'd made. He should have come up here alone and just bought her something himself, fuck the embarrassment factor.

Mrs Conroy scrutinized them both again. "You are bound to get on with Seth's mum, having such similar taste in accessories."

Great, just great. How the hell do I get out of this?

A moment later the two women were chuckling together and he peered at them. Whatever Lily had said to the other woman, had done the trick. Mrs Conroy blinked at him like a contented cat. "Your mother is very proud of you and what you do, Seth. I doubt she tells you enough, but…I just thought I'd mention it. Her only regret is that you don't have time for a proper family life. I'm sure she'll be delighted when she meets Lily." She winked conspiratorially, as if she'd approved Lily and would put in a good word for her.

Surreal. Seth wasn't sure how to handle this; it was way beyond his experience. And his temper was getting worse by the moment.

Lily seemed to notice and pulled into action before he did, shaking Mrs Conroy's hand. "We'd better make a move. It's been lovely meeting you. I could listen to your lovely Welsh accent all day. Seth's isn't so strong, what with living in London, although I still hear it in there. It's a beautiful accent." She looked at him with sparkling eyes.

Did she really think that? Seth didn't have long to consider it because he found himself ensconced in a brief perfumed hug from Mrs Conroy. He tried to clear his fogged brain. *Think, dammit.*

"I look forward to next time, Seth."

"Unit next time, you never saw us this time, right?"

His old teacher stared up at him; her eyes shrewd and assessing. Then she nodded, and was gone, disappearing into the nearby library.

Chaos management. His job shouldn't be about chaos management. It should be about rigorous procedures that were strictly adhered to. As they walked away he faced up to the fact that bringing Lily out was a mistake, another one. His judgement was shot to hell. He'd left a high profile witness unguarded and unsupervised, for what? A matter of life or death? No. Women's underwear. Jesus Christ.

He knew he was walking down the road too fast for Lily and that she was struggling to keep up, but he couldn't help himself. He kept one hand on her arm, determined to get this over with. *Get back to the witness. No more risks.*

"Seth, you're not annoyed are you? I had to let her think I was your girlfriend. If I hadn't, she'd have kept quizzing you."

Unbelievable. He ground to a halt turned to face her and grasped her by the upper arms. Looking into her eyes, he could see that she really thought that's what was annoying him. Everything about this was dangerous, and the bottom line was she was far too attractive to him and that was why he was functioning so badly. "You told her your name, for fuck's sake!"

Lily looked as if she had slapped him. "Oh. I'm sorry, I didn't think—"

"No, you didn't," he interrupted.

"Well I'm sorry, this is all new to me and..." She frowned. "Back up a minute, what the hell difference does it make if she knows my name anyway? It's Adrian who is the important one."

Seth groaned aloud with frustration. "She's a wily sort, and she knows me. Bringing a woman like you home is never going to happen, that's what will raise her suspicions that you're a witness."

The colour was draining from her face. "Look, I know you would rather I wasn't here, and I've made mistakes, but there is no need to be so rude about it."

Seth cursed aloud. "I didn't mean I don't want you here, you're..." He struggled to find the appropriate words, and then struggled to come to terms with the words that popped into his head. "You're a great girl, Lily."

He loosened his grip on her shoulders. She looked upset and that frustrated him even more. "My parents accept my job takes over my life. Annie Conroy is very close to my mother. She knows what I do for a living. We shouldn't even be out in public, and now there's a danger that she'll start passing her suspicion on in hushed whispers and soon everyone in the town will know your name. If your name is announced on TV, the connection will be made. All of this puts Adrian in danger because there is a connection between the two of you, and he doesn't need that kind of attention."

"Okay, I'm sorry. It was a mistake, all right!" Her lips tightened for a moment and she looked sorry she'd spoken. "Oh, crap! I keep saying and doing the wrong thing today," she blurted, shaking her head.

That rueful, annoyed face didn't look right on her. He wanted it gone. What the hell was wrong with him? He shouldn't even be thinking about stuff like that, it was way beyond his role here. A bit of emotional support, yes, but this sot of...caring, was above the call of duty. Too bad, he wanted to make her happy. Then he noticed that people were staring at them from across the street as they walked by. Shit. This was a small town, and gossip spread like wildfire. So much for keeping a low profile and not drawing attention, they were arguing in the middle of the street.

"Jesus Christ, you're making my job more difficult than it has ever been, and that is no small thing, believe me." He couldn't help glaring at her. "You need to understand that I would lay down my life for Adrian, and it's my job. I've left him up there at the house alone and I'm here with you, breaking cover to buy you fancy underwear because you're such a bloody pain in the arse."

Lily straightened up. Narrowing her eyes, she pulled out of his grasp.

At least she didn't look hurt anymore, which was a bloody relief.

Swivelling his head, he tried to get his bearings. They were two doors from the women's underwear shop. "Come on, let's get you this bloody underwear and get out of here."

Chapter Fourteen

Lily had learnt more about Seth in the past three hours than she had in the whole of the past three days, and yet she felt further away from him than ever. Sometimes, when he'd made love to her, it felt as if he was pouring his soul into her, and now — a chasm. Back at the house there was such a vibrant connection between them. It wasn't just the sex, not just the things they had done with Adrian, but beyond that, like he really cared. Other times, like today, she couldn't say or do the right thing. What was it about him? And — more to the point — why did she keep the ballsing it up with him?

"Good morning." The shop assistant stepped out from behind the glass display cabinet that doubled as a counter top. "Is there something specific I can help you with today?"

"Thank you, we're just browsing." Lily ventured deeper into the shop, but her attention was still with Seth, her mind running with all the things that had been said. She was just a nuisance to him, and it shouldn't hurt, but it did.

He was walking alongside her but looking beyond, through the window, his brow drawn down, and a horribly serious expression on his face. Was he still annoyed about his mother's friend? She'd never seen him so obviously flummoxed, and she felt bad. She'd gone along with it partly for fun, to see what he said, and that was wrong, he'd made that well and truly obvious. It had been a bit of a laugh, and now she regretted it.

As she walked through the shop, she noticed that there wasn't a practical piece of underwear to be seen. This was a full-on exotic lingerie shop, and as her gaze ran over the displays of satin, lace, and frippery of all kinds, her fingers itched to make the items hers.

Then she caught sight of a price tag, and gulped. The last thing she needed was to run up a big credit card bill, but then she glanced his way. She'd never had two men wanting to see her in her new undies before, and probably never would again. Wasn't that a good enough excuse to labour the credit card somewhat?

That's when she noticed he'd glanced back from the window and he was staring at the underwear as well, his eyebrows slightly lifted, his head titled back as if he'd suddenly found himself in a situation that he couldn't comprehend. The look on his face was too funny, and she had to bite her lip, the tension in her dissipating a tad. Perhaps she could ease him away from his bad mood with some of the sexy underwear? It wouldn't be easy, but Lily was willing to try anything, to hell with the expense.

Scanning the nearby table, she lifted a handful of lace and held it up. "What about this, do you like it?" She shimmied the flimsy one-piece in front of her chest, and then waggled her finger through the open crotch.

Glazed eyed, he stared at the lace teddy, and then shook his head slowly, sighing deeply like a man coming to terms with his burden. "I knew you were trouble the moment I saw you, and you just seem to keep hammering that fact home."

"You don't like it?"

"Of course I do, especially on you. Buy whatever you want." Peering at her, looking perplexed, he leant in and whispered in her ear. "I'm sorry I shouted. I'm just trying to do my job."

She lowered her hand to the table, underwear included, dreams of show time forgotten for a moment. Yes, she had lost focus; she'd shoved the dark side out of her mind and let the good stuff fill it. There was a killer out there, and Adrian — who she cared about deeply — was his target.

"I have that item in your size." The assistant's voice came from somewhere behind her.

Lily nearly shook her head, regretting that she had even dragged Seth there. "Thank you," she said quickly and flipped through a rail of garments with unseeing eyes.

It wasn't that she had forgotten Adrian's circumstances — how could she forget the sounds of that gunshot and the drama that had followed. She'd just got wrapped up in the situation between the three of them, the dynamic, and she'd happily let the rest take a back seat. Adrian was trying to do the right thing by standing up in a court, no matter how dangerous. She stared over at Seth's back, aching for him to be beside her again, his hand holding hers. *I'm wrapped up in him, too.*

She took a deep, unsteady breath, bracing herself to be hurt, badly. If today had proved anything it was that she was clueless, and the fun they'd shared was precious and sweet and hotter than hell, but it was also tenuous and transitory and she had to face up to that fact.

He turned away from the window and looked across at her, powerful shoulders broadening even before her eyes. His eyebrows were drawn down. She readied herself to leave, feeling ready to walk out that door and keep walking all the way back to London and her own life, no matter how dull. "Let's go."

Seth walked back to her, stopping her in her tracks, his arm around her waist.

Her heart beat wildly. She was ready to push his hand away, but couldn't. Forcing herself to meet his gaze, she found contrition there in his expression.

"Buy that...thing," he said, gesturing at the lace teddy she'd previously had in her hand. Snatching up a couple of pairs of exotic knickers from the table display, he shoved them into her hand. "Those too, just hurry up about it."

Her eyes stung with the threat of tears and she blinked them away, refusing to give in to it. His expression was still tense, and he didn't make contact with her, but it was enough. She nodded, relieved. At least she knew he wanted her to wear them, he wanted to see her in them. Silly though she knew it was, her body warmed through again, gladly.

Seth groped in his pocket, pulled out his wallet and slid her a wad of notes.

"It's okay," she said, "I can pay."

He shook his head. "No, I'll pay."

There was an emphatic tone to his voice, and the comment came out much louder than he meant, she was sure of it. "But...I can afford it."

"For god's sake, Lily," he declared, loudly, "it's my fault you don't have any decent underwear!"

The assistant dropped the display she was working on and stared over at them before she bent to retrieve it.

Lily looked at him, and now she was the one who was lifting her eyebrows. What with the prim Mrs Conroy and her remarks about Sunday school teaching, and then this, they were causing quite a stir in Conwy. "That's very chivalrous of you, Seth, but I have my credit card."

Seth grasped her hand, holding her in against him, and then whispered close against her ear. "You must use cash, sweetheart. Cards can be tracked. If you use your card now that can pinpoint your location for someone who knows how to work the system."

Someone like another cop, a cop who was working for the man who Adrian was testifying against. When his message hit home, she felt as if they were finally coming to an understanding of each other. This was hard for her, but it was for him too. "Right, of course. Sorry, I didn't think."

He nodded his head at her. "Be safe, okay." He pushed the cash into her hand. "And hurry, please." With that, his attention was once more on the street outside.

He was constantly worried about Adrian, and about her, too. Lily took a deep breath, and then smiled over at the assistant who was watching them. She tried to look normal—whatever normal might be. Given her current, unexpected circumstances she'd lost touch with normal. Laden with feminine guilt, she clutched the underwear that he'd liked and took her stash to the cash register.

"You've made some lovely choices," the assistant commented as she began to scan the price tags.

Lily nodded.

"We have matching accessories for this item." It was the black lace one-piece. The assistant reached onto the shelf behind her and lifted lace topped stockings.

"You have to have the full set." It was Seth, and he was back at her side.

Lily nodded, and the two items were added to the bag.

Moments later they were on their way. They walked to the car double-time.

Seth didn't say a word. He kept one hand under her elbow all times.

"I'm sorry about the credit card business," she said, as they reached the car and they were out of earshot of anyone else around. "I should have been more...cautious. I feel clueless."

"You are clueless, but that's no bad thing. I'd hate to be shagging a woman who knew about this sort of stuff, that wouldn't bode well." He was joking, trying to put her at her ease, but he also turned her to face him, and this time it didn't skip her attention that he was shielding her body as they stood outside the car.

Looking deep into her eyes, he studied her. "This is a difficult situation. It's unfortunate you had to be dragged into it, but my duty is to protect." His hand cupped her jaw, and she turned and kissed his palm. "I've been doing this job a long time, maybe too long. It's lonely work. You're good to be around, Lily, you're a breath of fresh air. You've made this...easier on me." After a long moment, during which she could scarcely breathe because of the way he looked at her, he sighed and his glance flickered away. "But I can't ever totally forget why we're here."

She found it strangely hard to speak, but she wanted to. Difficult as this was, she wanted it, because she felt more connected to him than she had at any point in their time together, and she didn't want the moment to escape. She rested her hand against his chest. "I'm sorry that I wasn't more aware of that. I should have known. I'm having fun with you and Adrian, I can't deny that, but deep down I'm worried about the stuff I had to leave behind. I should have been more aware of what you and Adrian are dealing with too."

His gaze locked back on hers. "You couldn't possibly know how all this works, how it affects someone like Adrian, or me." He stroked her hair. "I don't expect you to know, but sometimes I can't be exactly how I want to be, with you." Again he paused. It was as if he wanted to say more, but couldn't decide how much or what to say.

Lily knew better than to push him. He'd said enough. He'd revealed more about himself inside that one minute than he had in three days. She stared up at his handsome face, her emotions tangling. "I'm sorry about the lingerie."

"I'm not." Smiling sardonically, as if brooding on some inner thoughts, he shook his head, and nodded his head at the passenger door.

She turned to the vehicle and her hand went to the door handle automatically, but he closed his over it, making her pause. "In this job," he continued, standing close at her back as she waited for him to open the door for her. "I signed up for it all, to protect or die. When we are outside the safe house I can't afford to be distracted. Duty has to come first when you're protecting witnesses, and that means both of you."

Every part of her back was protected by his body, just as he had in London outside Adrian's office, and it was so subtle but so obvious that she had to bite her lip to stop herself from responding.

The car door clicked open. She lifted the handle and then glanced over her shoulder at him. "Thank you."

"I did wonder there for a while, but you're worth the trouble, every ounce of it." The teasing expression was returning to his face, and the set of his mouth indicated he was accepting the way she was, that he might even enjoy being kept on his toes. With the lightest of strokes he touched her face.

It was so brief it made her yearn for more, but she didn't hassle him. Instead she got into the car quietly, clutching her lingerie bag to her chest as she settled into the seat.

The thunk of his door shutting locked them together in the intimate space, and yet the journey back to the house was silent. The landscape along the meandering road that had fascinated her on their outward journey seemed almost therapeutic this time around. Why, because she needed the space? Glancing over at him, she realised this had knocked her back a peg. She'd been gung-ho on the danger, the sexy set-up, and the fire between the three of them. When had she got to be so bound up in herself and her needs? Back in her days of not being able to do her duty as a nurse, it was always because she thought she was fighting for the good cause, and for the rights of the patient. Then again, she'd never been involved in anything like this before, and yet it had been so obvious and she kicked herself for not being more aware, for not making it easier for him. She'd got carried away on the dynamic and forgotten the reason why they were all stuck out there together. Seth had to be stressed out of his eyeballs, and she was busy having fun.

As they closed on the valley where the hotel was located, he changed down the gears and then he moved his hand to her thigh, squeezing her. It was reassuring. She was relieved to see the *Hafod Y Coed* sign, and silently read the words with even more interest now that she knew it was his childhood home.

"Does it all look okay?" she asked as they pulled up at the back of the building, and her stomach was knotted.

"Looks good so far." He smiled her way. He didn't say more than that, but she felt as if they had met each other half way in understanding.

When they walked into the hallway, she had the overwhelming urge to shout out to Adrian, to be sure, but Seth beat her to it.

"We're back."

"I'll put the kettle on." Adrian's voice reached them from the kitchen area.

"He's fine."

Thank god. The sense of relief she felt made her light-headed, the knot in her stomach unravelling. If anything had happened to Adrian while they had been gone she'd never have been able to forgive herself. She dumped the lingerie bag on the hall stand, resenting it all of a sudden. Luxury items they were, in more ways than one. It was a luxury she truly could have done without. She could have made do.

Seth's hand on her shoulder drew her back. He was right there, his reassuring presence close against her. Out of the corner of her eye, she saw him pick up the bag. He held it out to her. "Take it. I want you to wear it, all of it, tonight."

Lily stared down at the bag he held against her, unable to move.

"It's okay, take it, please."

Her hand closed over his on the handle of the bag.

His head lowered alongside hers. Mouth against her ear, he nipped hear ear lobe between his teeth. Deliciously painful, yet poignant and arousing, it was a connection she couldn't deny. Breath sucked into her lungs, her chest expanding.

"Lily, you'll look so bloody good. I didn't mean to be a tyrant, I'm sorry. I want to see you wearing it, all of it." His mouth rested against her cheek, soft as a sigh.

Lily savoured it, her whole body attuned to his. Aching for him deeply, she blinked back the emotion before she turned her face to his, looking up at him.

His expression was still overcast and yet he looked at her as if he wanted her to understand, as if he was requesting it, earnestly, and it was the first-time she had ever seen him looking at either her or Adrian that way. It was like he was letting her in. Her heart knotted in her chest. In the beginning she had thought him cold, brutal, and demanding, but it was simply because he had to be that way.

She went to speak, and then the sound of the kettle whistling madly reached them. She pulled a froth of lace out of the bag, and held it to her chest. "Do you think he'll like it?"

Oh, how her heart ached. She felt as if she was asking permission, asking for him to let Adrian be involved. And yet...neither had said anything about how things stood between them, or about Adrian and his role in bringing the three of them together. Seth had grown more intimate with her over the past day or so, but what did that really mean? Her emotions were intricately bound up with both men now. Seth's guiding hand was crucial, and she wanted Seth's approval of the way things were panning out.

But Seth just smiled, long slow. "I know he will. He'll love it. We both will."

For Lily, that comment meant the whole world. She reached up, kissed him on the mouth and nodded. "Let's make it an evening to remember."

Chapter Fifteen

Lily took a sip of her wine, and put the glass down. She'd thought she would need it, but she didn't. She was already on a natural high and she really wanted to do this. It had been a fantasy for so long, to have a man who she wanted – and who wanted her –watching as she stripped and danced, just for him. Andrea had teased her about it and then bought her a stripping technique DVD for Christmas. They'd watched it for a laugh, but Lily had played it on her own, too, while she ran her hands over her body and flicked her hips from side to side, imagining her dream man sitting in front of her, hard and ready while she strutted her stuff like a professional exotic dancer.

Now she had two dream men to dance for, and they both *were* dream men, in different ways. She smiled to herself as she thought that. Yes, in different ways. Seth was so full on, so black and white in his opinions, and yet so mysterious at the same time. She craved his dangerous edge, his sureness about going after what he wanted. Adrian was the more subtle seducer, the everyday guy who could reveal his blatantly deviant sexuality as and when it pleased him. He was the one who pushed her buttons at the crucial moment, the one who made her confident enough to take them both on. The fact that they both wanted her was such a turn on. She could see it in their eyes, feel it in their touches.

It might be just this place and the set up, she reminded herself, but whatever it was she wanted every moment of it.

When she'd gone to get ready they had both whispered encouragement. Adrian gave her a long glance that positively smouldered, while Seth looked as if he was about to strip her right there and then, not waiting for the show.

The sound of rock music reached her across the hall when she opened her door, and she smiled. Taking a deep breath, she checked her outfit one last time. She'd chosen to wear the lacy one-piece with the open crotch that she'd teased Seth with in the shop. The matching stockings the assistant had suggested really set it off. The teddy was covered over by her thigh-length coat for now—for the slow reveal. Everything was in place, and she strode across the hall and stepped through the door in to the lounge. Their conversation ceased as she entered the room, and both men turned and stared at her.

"Here she is," Adrian said. They'd been waiting.

Seth lounged back in his chair expectantly. "You are one lucky man," he said to Adrian, nodding her way.

Adrian grinned, not taking his eyes off her. "I am, but then so are you."

Seth lifted one shoulder in a kind of shrug. He still didn't think she wanted him as much as she wanted Adrian. Lily chuckled, and when she heard the throaty sensuality in her own laughter the heat inside her multiplied.

Adrian was still grinning, but he was also shaking his head as he took in her ensemble. It was the same coat and high heels that she had worn to his office that first night. She didn't have a lot of choice on that score. The difference was that the thigh-length trench coat was belted, making it ride up, and the tops of her stockings were showing. She'd borrowed a black trilby that she'd found on the hall coat stand, to complete her look.

The door clicked shut behind her. She took that as her cue. "You like?"

"Oh yes." Adrian's eyes glittered, and they exchanged a glance of raw passion.

Moving her hips to the music, she stepped across the room, toying with the belt on the coat, turning this way and that to give them a good look at the stockings.

"I want to see what you've got under the coat," Seth commented.

"All in good time," she responded over her shoulder, and then stalked over to a nearby chair and dragged it behind her as she walked back to them. She planted one heel on the chair; hips still moving to the sound of the rock music, and smoothed her stockings up the length of her legs. The way Adrian's eyes widened indicated he was getting an eyeful of the open crotch. He groaned. She changed feet, smoothing the other stocking.

"Take pity on me, "Adrian begged, hands out in her direction. "I'm a condemned man, please come closer."

"You're not the condemned man, and don't you forget it," she responded. Eyeballing him expectantly, she faced him and undid the belt, letting the coat almost fall open. "Promise?"

"Okay, I promise."

She dropped the coat the floor. A moment later she leaned over him, putting her hands on his shoulders and kissing him, just to be sure that he was paying attention.

He held his hands up as she straightened, his gaze covering her from top to bottom, taking in the sheer black lace bodysuit, stockings and heels. She could already see that he was hard inside his jeans. Swaying from side to side she carefully kept her thighs together, keeping the secret of the open crotch a while longer. When she glanced Seth's way, she knew he hadn't forgotten. He was practically drooling.

Happier than she'd ever been, she let the music invade her senses—let it lead her hips and arms. Secure in the knowledge that both of them cared for her in different ways, she was in a safe environment to really unleash her secret fantasy. She felt powerfully female, rich to overflowing with it. Dancing until her skin was slick and pumping and grinding was what her body craved next. She straddled the chair she'd set out in between them, and folded her arms across the back support.

Both men reacted. Seth leant forward, eyes blazing at her. Adrian exhaled, loudly, staring pointedly between her thighs. "When you went out for underwear, I didn't picture this."

"*Lingerie*," Seth explained. "That's what it's called."

Decadent and empowered, Lily blew them both a kiss. Cool air tickled her bare pussy lips, and she rocked her hips back and forth, her body eager for contact and a different kind of dance. Her pussy was slick with need, her body anticipating the hot action that would follow.

When she stood up, Seth followed and stepped behind her.

He ran his hands down her front, teasing her breasts through the thin lacy covering. Then he pulled her into his arms, giving her an idea how hard he was. His cock was upright between her buttocks. "We want you. You're driving us crazy."

"Is that a bad thing?"

"Depends how far you push it. I've got a stonking erection and I'd put money on the fact Adrian has as well."

Breathless, and dizzy with arousal, she tipped her head back, resting back in his embrace. "That's music to my ears, because I'm all fired up."

She pulled free, and stepped over to Adrian. Tossing her hair, she turned her back and swung her hips from side to side over his lap. He kept his hands on the arms of the chair for maybe twenty seconds, and then they were on her instead, one on her hip, the other reaching into the open crotch of her outfit to touch her damp slit.

When she looked his way, Seth shoved his hand into his pocket, pulling a handful of condoms and offering them to her. She snatched one from his hand and opened it, turning to face Adrian. She bent and undid his fly, purring her approval when his cock poked out of his jeans, long and hard and ready to be ridden. She was bent over at the waist, and behind her Seth groaned heavily. He had his fingers in the open crotch, roving up and down over her slick folds and the swollen nub of her clit.

She had to bite her lip, and grasp the arms of Adrian's chair for a moment, steadying herself. Her heels didn't feel strong enough to support her wobbly legs any more, but she willed herself to carry on, tearing the condom packet open, even while Seth moved one finger inside her. She was so wet that the movement of his finger made a sound. Seth muttered something incoherent and pushed another finger inside, nudging against the tender, sensitive place on the front wall of her sex.

Adrian's cock jerked against his belly, and his hands moved on her lace-covered breasts. Sensation swamped her. She clamped on Seth's fingers, and resisted the urge to ride them. "Let me get this bloody condom on, Seth."

"Yes, let her get the bloody condom on," Adrian said.

The humour of the moment forced her to breathe, breaking the tension.

"Sorry guys. It was just so tempting." He removed his fingers, mercifully, a moment later, and she found her hips steadied by his strong hands.

"That's good." She got the condom into position on the head of Adrian's cock, and slowly rolled it on, marvelling at how hard he was. Her sex ached to be filled with him.

Standing straight she turned to Seth, grabbed him with her hands around his head and kissed him passionately. Then she eased backwards and sat on to Adrian's lap, her hand guiding his erection inside her aching sex.

The head of his cock buoyed up against her cervix and she rocked her hips, her spine straightening, her mouth open in a rush of pleasure, a loud moan escaping her. Adrian spread his legs wide, giving her space to stand between his knees, and she lifted up and down, smiling up at Seth as she did so.

"Let me see what you've got," she teased, and nodded at his zipper, where the fabric was tight and bulging under the strain of his erection.

He didn't need any more encouragement, his hands undoing his belt in a flash, his cock pushing between the buttons on his jeans. He rode it with one hand while he watched her rising and falling on Adrian's lap. "You are so hot. I could come just watching you right now."

The surge of female power that swept up through her when he said that made her stronger. "That's not good enough." She flashed her eyes at him. "I want your cock as well."

He swallowed, visibly. His hand was still riding his shaft but he moved it slower, as if he was drawing out the pleasure and forcing himself to take his time. "How are you going to manage that then?"

His eyebrows were lifting, one corner of his mouth, too.

"Oh, I've had lots of ideas, believe me." She winked as she bore down onto Adrian.

He cursed.

He was wedged deep and she rocked her hips so that he rubbed in all the right places.

His fingers ran down her back, and she knew he was wired to let loose, but it was not going to happen yet, she wanted more. Then his hands ran down her spine, lower, to where the back of her open crotch began, and he followed the crease between her buttocks. When his fingers stroked the tight button of her anus, she moaned longingly and nodded her head.

"Open another condom," she said to Seth.

Silently, he did as instructed, but when he went to put it on she stopped him and guided his cock to her mouth, kissing it before taking it into her mouth for a moment. When he cursed aloud, she sucked him harder, feeling wicked, deviant, and able to take on the world. She moved it against the roof of her mouth several times before she pulled back. "Put it on. I want you both."

Lifting away from Adrian's cock, she ran her fingers over his sheathed cock. It was slippery with her juices. She could take it. Easing it back to her anus, she felt Adrian grasp it, and she held the arms of the chair as she worked her bottom against the pressure, relaxing enough to ease it inside.

"Fuck," her head dropped back, her arms straining.

Adrian steadied her with one hand on her back, and she moved again, resting the back of her thighs against the edge of the seat between his legs, she leant forward to accommodate him. His cock seemed even larger and harder as it eased into her forbidden passage, and then she quivered, opened, and took him in.

Adrian grasped her around the waist, and drew her upper body back so that she had her back to his chest. Pure, ragged sensation shot the length of her spine, and her mouth parted. Seth was on his knees between her legs, stroking her splayed pussy. The pleasure that pulsed from his fingertips entwined with the intense, almost painful sensation at her rear, making her cry out and pant for breath.

Seth rolled his condom on, and moved the crown of his cock into her splayed opening, pushing inside.

"Oh, oh. So much." Her voice was garbled as she tried to get the words out. Her body was primed for this, but the intense and various stimuli swamping her groin made it difficult to breathe.

"Can you take it?" Seth asked, his voice low. "Just tell me to stop, sweetheart, if you can't."

"It's almost too much," she said, and it came out on a blast of breath. "Almost."

Seth braced himself with one hand and the armchair, the line of his mouth tight as he waited for her word, her command.

"More." Her head rolled back, dropping against Adrian's shoulder and he kissed her neck. Seth shifted again, the head of his cock wedged just inside her. "Give me more, slowly," she instructed, emphasising that final word.

"You got it, whatever you want." He gave it to her an inch at a time; slow, so slowly but inexorably stretching her to take his gloriously hard cock. Whimpering, her fingers locked on the arms of the chair, the sensory overload taking her over.

"Sorry," she breathed, to Adrian, "I can't move, can't move."

He gave a husky laugh against her ear. "No need to move." His hands stroked her breasts from behind, outlining them through the lace. "We can do that for you."

His hands moved lower. Cupping her bottom he manipulated her easily, shifting her position ever so slightly. The reverberations weren't so slight—the two upright shafts inside her made her nether regions hum with sensation, heat swamping her.

Moaning loudly, she grasped for something solid and found Seth's shoulders. When she met his stare, she could see he was still pacing himself. Her entire skin grew damp with expectation. Swallowing hard she nodded, indicating she could take more.

He found his rhythm, thrusting in and out of her slippery channel, the muscles in his arms and neck cording.

"Oh fuck," she cried out, "this is intense."

"Uhuh," murmured Adrian, "and I can feel Seth's cock fucking you."

Seth shook his head at Adrian's remark, but his cock seemed to get even harder at the suggestion. Lily moaned, indicating that she shared the intensity — the absolute poignancy of their proximity inside her.

At her back, Adrian shifted, sliding out and then in again, and fire rocketed up the length of her spine. Her body went supine, overloaded with stimuli. The two cocks so close inside her, sliding against each other — she was gone on it. Her sex grasped the length of Seth's shaft, her clit throbbing wildly. A hot fist closed around her core. The first spasm hit just as Seth's cock nudged her centre. Her clit went tight as a drum pounding with release, while her sex rippled and clenched the glorious erections that filled her, hot juices spilling from her sex.

"That feels so damn good," Adrian whispered, holding her steady from beneath.

Seth nodded. "Never a truer word spoken, my friend."

She lifted her head and locked eyes with him.

He thrust deep again, then paused. "Never felt anything like this."

Her chest grew tight, her hips rocking forward in response to his words.

His eyes flashed shut, then opened. They were filled with warning. "Move like that again and I'm going to come."

"I want you to. I want you both to come, inside me." She wrapped her hands around his upper arms, the muscle there hard and tight as she rocked her hips and he thrust harder and faster, his cock arching. Tension was fast building again, riffing on the pleasure of her previous release, making her dizzy. Drunk on it, a breathless, disbelieving laugh escaped her open mouth.

Adrian exhaled, loudly. He pulled on her lace-covered nipples, then his cock went rigid, like steel. She felt the release, his cock jerking three times. Seth grunted and she knew he could feel it too. His back arched, his broad shoulders flexing as he thrust and came.

She felt his cock right at her sensitive centre. A blitz of sensation hit her. The lights seemed to dim and then get overly bright, and she clutched at the arms of the chair. Her sex tightened and released, and pleasure exploded through her, needling up her back until it washed right over her and swept up round her neck, making her nipples sting, her breath rasping in her throat.

Her body wavered. Adrian had pulled free.

"It's okay; I've got you, sweetheart."

It was Seth, and she realised he was holding her, encouraging her to put her arms around his neck. Gratefully, she sighed and rested her arms around him wearily, her body too heavy to move. Her heart brimmed, the rush from her orgasm dancing with her emotions. "Good job you're here, because you're going to have to carry me to the bed."

"Me too," Adrian said.

Seth laughed at that, and she ate it up with her eyes, because he looked so happy, and she'd never seen him look quite that way before.

Chapter Sixteen

Lily awoke when the central heating kicked up a notch. Blinking, she looked over at the bedside clock. It was seven. The morning was overcast. A moment later she carefully extracted herself from her spot on the bed, where she was comfortably ensconced between he warm, supine bodies of the two men.

Standing beside the bed she looked back at them. Deep in sleep, they gravitated towards each other as if looking for her warmth, not realising she had gone. Any standoffishness about touching each other was slowly evaporating. That felt good. In fact, that felt like quite an achievement.

Slipping on a pair of socks, she reached into the carrier that she'd left hanging over the dressing chair and pulled out a pair of her new fancy undies. Opting to borrow a large sweatshirt as a dressing gown, she slid it over her head, breathing in the scent of male cologne. It was loose on her, covering her to mid thigh. She'd seen both men wearing it, and assumed it was Seth's. They were time sharing it, a bit like they were time sharing her.

They slept soundly still, so she wandered to the kitchen and put the kettle on. While her tea brewed, she looked out of the window longingly. It was a crisp winter morning, with icing sugar frost on the grass. The grounds looked beautiful and she longed to be out there, exploring. It was a crime to be here in the beautiful Welsh countryside and not engage with it. Her mind flitted back to when Seth had let her out there.

Two minutes wouldn't hurt, surely? Taking her mug of tea with her, she walked quietly to the hallway and opened up the control box, remembering how Seth had switched of the alarm for her to visit the patio the day before. The alarm was clearly marked and she clicked it off, then went into the sitting-room, and opened the French windows. The brisk air hit her lungs, exhilarating her, and she stepped out onto the patio, looking out across the sky. There was a glare behind the scudding clouds, and it made her want to walk for miles. Even if she could, would she feel free?

Deep inside she recognised that this was more than a safe house, this was her love nest. Her emotions were well and truly tangled and even if she was able to leave now, what they had shared was inescapable. She'd bonded with these two, here in this safe house, and even if she'd wanted to break free she couldn't. Even if the opportunity truly was here, because she didn't want to leave them. Was it Stockholm syndrome? No, she'd wanted Adrian through his words alone. He'd proved just as attractive in real life, and even more easy-going than she had thought. And Seth—well, she'd practically jumped him the minute she saw him, back in London, and that was before any of this locked-up-together business. Being forced to be here this way had only made things evolve quicker than they might have in ordinary life. Would they have all bonded this way, as a threesome, in ordinary life? Maybe not, maybe circumstances had allowed that side of things to happen more readily than it might have done.

She could hear a bird twittering from beyond the patio, where the bare limbs of the trees meshed together in her vision. The cold, frost-covered stones beneath her feet iced through her borrowed socks. With her hands wrapped around her mug to keep them warm and Seth's long sweatshirt draped over her fingers, she stepped from one foot to the other, resisting the cold for as long as she could before she had to go back inside.

I want to come back here, in the summer, she thought. It was a beautiful place, and she'd never forget it. Never forget this time she'd had with Adrian and Seth, either. How could she? It was all her fantasies and more. Her love life had been on hold for a while, until she and Andrea had got the business up and running. That's why she had turned to the internet for some fun. Before that, in her nursing days, things had never been easy. She'd always been too involved in her job. Relationships had been all about blowing off steam and they hadn't lasted long. The nearest thing she'd had to a true love had been back in her college days, when she'd had a relationship with one man throughout. After they'd graduated, geographical distance had made that one slowly dissolve. And now she had two lovers, two good men. Sighing wistfully, her mind wandered.

They'd been flung together, but they'd clicked — all three of them had clicked into place with each other. Strange, but true. However, she doubted either of them would be interested in seeing her again, after all of this was over.

Adrian was having fun, but this wasn't what he'd signed up for and deep down she felt guilty about that. Seth...well, Seth was a different kettle of fish altogether. She suspected he was just keeping himself amused, or keeping them all amused, or something. Whatever, he'd made it clear he wasn't taking it seriously. Even so, she couldn't help wondering what it would be like to be with them both under normal circumstances. Would it be the same? Maybe not, but she'd like to find out. She saw Adrian teasing Seth, Seth being put out, but silently accepting the more gentle man's opinion. Like a subtle exchange between bonded friends. The fact that they did it in front of her was a strange and unexpected aphrodisiac. Breathing deep, she savoured the image, locking it into her heart where she would treasure it, always

Somewhere behind her, a twig snapped.

Seth? She glanced over her shoulder, but not quite quickly enough.

She saw a fast moving figure dressed in black, and a flash of ice-blond hair.

Her mug crashed to the ground.

A large, oppressive hand fell over her mouth, and her body was crushed in a death-grip. When she tried to cry out, her breath was choked out of her lungs.

* * * *

Adrian woke up, and immediately knew that Lily wasn't close by. He sat up and checked. Seth was lying a foot or so away, and there was a space in between them. The door was ajar and cold air funnelled through it. He listened for

Lily, but couldn't hear anything. Something told him this wasn't right.

"Wake up." With one hand on Seth's shoulder, he whispered the words.

Seth lifted his head off the pillow. "Huh?"

"Wake up. I have a bad feeling."

Seth was upright inside a heartbeat. "Where's Lily?"

"I don't know. Woke up and she was gone." He shook his head. "Not in the bathroom, and I can't hear her."

Seth was on his feet pulling his jeans on. Adrian did the same. Seth pulled his gun out of his boot, where he deposited it each night, and then shoved his feet into the boots. Adrian was just about to reach for a T-shirt, when a sound reached them, a shattering sound, and a muffled scream.

"Outside," Seth said through gritted teeth. He stalked to the hallway, half dressed, gun in hand. Adrian followed, but at the doorway Seth turned and stopped him, pushing him back into the room. "You stay here, and lock the door behind me. Go into the bathroom and lock that door as well, and don't come out until I tell you to."

Adrian shook his head, moving forward against the hand Seth had up against his chest. "It's my fault that she's here at all. There is no way I'm going to do anything else but come and help."

Seth's eyes blazed. "The hell you are. You are my primary witness. It is my duty to make sure you are safe, even if that means putting my life on the line. Deal with it."

Adrian swallowed, but it was Lily out there. To hell with Carlisle and the court case. "It's Lily." He locked eyes with Seth and they stood silently sparring, the tension soaring.

"I'll find her."

"I'll help."

They were squaring up to each other, but Seth shook his head. "I'm not above knocking you out cold to keep you down and safe."

"It's Lily," Adrian repeated, empathically, "and if you were me you couldn't just sit here and wait. Face it, as soon as you leave, I am following." The door could only be locked from the inside. Seth didn't respond to that one, unable to. Adrian continued quickly. "We're wasting time. I'll stay behind you, but you could really use a second pair of eyes right now."

"Jesus, you two are the most pain-in-the-arse witnesses I have ever experienced." Seth shook his head, his eyes flickering as he looked into the hallway. "See that you do stay back," he added over his shoulder, "and keep your eyes peeled."

In the hallway, the control box was open. Seth stared at it, muttering to himself. "This is my fault."

With his back against the wall, he moved slowly along hallway to the residents' lounge. Dipping his head inside, he held one hand up, indicating that Adrian wait. The cold air was definitely coming from that direction. A moment later, Seth moved into the doorway, cocked gun in front of him. Then he disappeared into the room.

When Adrian followed, he saw that the French windows were wide open, the open curtains lifting on the winter air. However, it was the silence, and not the cold, that made him shiver.

Seth quickly pointed at him, and then pointed behind the bar, indicating he take cover there. Adrian was unwilling, but Seth glared at him. He did as instructed, dropping to his knees behind the bar, whilst watching

Seth's manoeuvres over the edge. It occurred to him in a moment of extreme irony that there wasn't much point in keeping him protected right now, seeing as he didn't give a shit about anything but Lily's safety.

Seth hadn't even got close to the French windows when a shot rang out. Had they left the doors wide open like a trap? Adrian felt sick. The hairs on his back stood up. Was Lily even alive? He crushed the thought that it was otherwise.

The back of the bar ran up to the edge of the curtains, further along the room, where the casement window ended, and he headed in that direction. Seth had his back against the curtains, a few inches to the side of the open glass doors. From memory, Adrian recognised that he was against the wall flanking the French windows. "Nice try," Seth shouted, "but you seem to keep missing your targets."

Silence.

"You make me sick, Lavonne," Seth shouted, "selling out like this."

Seth knew the man? Confusion hit him, but he continued to creep along behind the bar, desperate to be sure that Lily was unharmed.

A gruff laugh came from beyond the window and then a muffled cry. *Lily?*

That sound fuelled him. He glanced at Seth. He was pinching his forehead, teeth gritted. Anger and regret poured out of him, and inside a heartbeat Adrian knew that his guardian was in love with her too.

"Give me Walsh," a voice shouted from beyond, "in exchange for the woman."

"Do it," Adrian hissed. "I'll go."

Seth shot him the blackest look he had ever seen, shaking his head. "Even if I could let you do that, it wouldn't help. Lily can identify him, as can I."

Adrian's hands fisted at his sides.

"Now why on earth would you do that?" Seth shouted back through the open doorway.

He'd managed to sound much more self-assured than he looked, Adrian noticed.

"All I needed is to keep the witness under *my* protection," the man outside responded, "until after the trial. You know it makes sense."

Seth's head went back against the wall. Adrian watched, wondering how he would respond. Adrian didn't even know the guy, and he didn't believe him. It was pretty obvious Seth didn't believe it, either.

Rising up, Adrian took a chance, lifted the curtain and peaked out the casement window. He caught sight of them immediately. They were behind the largest of the nearby trees, some ten feet away from the open glass doors where Seth was standing. The man who'd been on the fire escape outside his office had Lily crushed against the tree, one hand over her mouth. The other held a gun to her head. She was alive, but who knew for how long? The bloke holding her looked as if he wanted to blow her away and then walk over here and shoot the lot of them. He was merely using her as a shield, and if he got brave, he wouldn't need that shield anymore.

Adrian had to swallow down the bile that rose in his throat. Forcing himself to take another glance, it occurred to him that if he had the gun, and knew how to use it, he could shoot the guy. From this angle, the bastard was pretty much totally exposed, while Lily was partly-obscured between his body and the tree.

Taking a deep steadying breath, he stepped back along the bar.

Waving frantically, he attracted Seth's attention. When Seth looked his way, he pointed at the edge of the curtain and beyond to where the tree was.

Seth's eyes flickered, and then he nodded. "You're scum, Lavonne," he called out. "Why would I even begin to believe in you and your so-called deal, tell me that?" After he'd shouted the question out through the open doors he darted across the room and levered himself over the bar.

Adrian stood close by as Seth moved into the position he'd vacated.

"Because you have no choice," came the response. "Carlisle's men are following me, you either do as I say, or you will all die."

Adrian's blood ran cold. More of them? He exchanged a glance with Seth.

Seth's jaw turned to granite. Then he was at the curtain, his gun easing into the gap.

Unease swamped Adrian. Would he be able to get a shot off without injuring Lily? It might take time, and meanwhile that guy out there was waiting for a response. Bracing himself, Adrian headed across the room and took up the position Seth had left. Adopting Seth's voice, he shouted out, "You're scum, Lavonne," repeating Seth's earlier remark.

"Fuck you, Jones," came the bitter response.

"Nice work." It was Seth, and Adrian caught the comment in the split-second before he heard the sound of shattering glass and a single shot rang out.

Please let her be safe. Please.

The sound of a woman's scream took away any last vestige of responsibility he had, and he darted out onto the patio, just in time to see the man's body slump away from the tree, blood staining his forehead. Lily was running in his direction, and he opened his arms and held her.

Her entire body was shaking and cold, her forehead damp with sweat, her face scratched. She stared up at him, eyes wild, confusion and fear filling them.

"You're safe, he's gone." Hushing her, soothing her, and holding her close, he thanked God. Seth pushed past and jogged over to check the body, removing the gun as he did so.

Seconds later they heard the distant noise of sirens, and a loud thrumming sound.

Seth joined them.

"I'm sorry," Lily whispered, looking at Seth, choking on her tears.

Seth didn't let her say more than that. Instead, he reached in to give her a passionate kiss on the mouth, hands wrapped around the back of her head, before nodding at the sky, where a police helicopter was moving in. "The cavalry," he commented with no small amount of irony. "I guess that email made it through after all. Better late than never, hey."

* * * *

It took a long time to give her statement, but the police woman who worked with Lily was patient and understanding. They'd wrapped a blanket around her, and someone brought her a sweet cup of tea.

Too much sugar, she thought, as she sipped it, not like Seth made it.

Everything had happened so quickly and it was hard to make sense of it all. She'd found herself being led inside the house by a police officer. They took her to the office, a room she'd only seen once or twice during her stay. When she glanced out the window there, she saw that there were police cars parked in the driveway, beyond Seth's Land Rover. It was local constabulary. The vehicles were marked 'police' in both English and Welsh.

Adrian had been led away when she was. She remembered his fingers slipping from hers, and hated it. They were safe, though. Even so, it felt like the world she had got used to over the last few days was being fractured, and there was an ache in her chest that just got heavier. The last she'd seen of Seth he was with a man in a shirt and tie who had arrived with others in the helicopter. The two embraced each other. Was that the boss, the one with the little girl Seth had sent the message to?

"You're doing well," the policewoman assured her. "Take a minute to have your tea. Once we've finished your statement, I'll arrange for you to be taken home."

"Thank you." Home? Where was home, now?

The police woman stepped out of the room for a moment, and Lily wrapped her hands around the mug, sipping the tea, taking strength from it.

Home was with Andrea, she reminded herself. Yes, with their business and their flat and all the pride and hard work that went with that. It would be good to see her friend, but at the same time Lily felt distanced from her life because so much had happened in the few days she'd spent with Adrian and Seth. She'd been opened to new experiences, and she felt enriched, both emotionally and sexually, after the time she'd spent with them.

If only I hadn't turned off the alarm, if only I hadn't gone out on the patio. Her mind kept flitting back to what had happened out there. They cared, and their actions showed her how much. That gave her strength.

When she was finally done and they let her leave the office, encouraging her to gather her things, she went to where she'd last seen them, the lounge, and looked there and beyond, on the patio. They'd gone. Her heart sank.

"Of course they've gone," she said to herself, feeling as if someone had pulled the earth from under her feet. "Gone to a new safe house, without me."

Her stomach clenched and her chest ached horribly. She hadn't even had a chance to thank them for what they'd done, for everything. She put her hand to her mouth, telling herself over and over again not to cry, but the tears came anyway.

Chapter Seventeen

"If you'd asked me, a month ago," Adrian commented, "what I thought living in a brand new show home might be like, I'd have assumed it would be luxurious." He stared at the rumpled sleeping bag on the sofa with a sense of wistfulness. "I feel like I can't touch anything. It's all so...beige."

Seth chuckled, glancing at the walls and the sparse but expensive furnishings. "Yes, so it is."

"I'll never want to see anything beige ever again."

"Agreed. " Seth nodded.

The pair of them were sprawled on the floor of the lounge area in the show home, which was located somewhere on a half built housing estate in Surrey. "You're doing well. Two more days and we're out of here."

"And I miss your Dad's bar," Adrian added.

"I know." Seth gave a rueful smile. "So do I." Then he shook his head. "That bar will hold legendary status, forevermore." They exchanged brief glances, reliving the moment.

"Good. Grandest bar I've ever been in. Nice drop of brandy, too." Adrian reached over to the chessboard that sat on the floor between them, replacing the pieces from the game they had shared earlier, and then glanced across at his friend and protector. "And that's not all I miss."

Seth's smile faded and he shot a warning glance. "Don't even go there."

Adrian shrugged. "I know you're thinking about her."

Seth scowled. "And you aren't?"

"Of course I am, but not in the same way you are."

"What's that supposed to mean?"

"You've fallen for her. I have too, but I was prepared for that to happen because of what we had shared online. Whereas, you didn't think you would get involved." He'd given a great deal of thought to how to broach this subject with Seth, and decided that head on was going to be the only way. "You thought it would be quick and easy, a bit of fun, no harm done. And now you can't forget her."

Seth across stared at him, dumbstruck. After a moment, he ran his hand along the stubble on his jaw. "No, I haven't fallen for her. Not possible." He paused, as if thinking it through, then continued — as Adrian had expected he would when he decided to raise the subject — giving excuses for the fact he was sitting there with a faraway look in his eyes. "I miss the female company, I can't deny that, and Lily was one hell of a special woman, but it was crazy, I mean...I don't usually get involved like that. It was a one-off. Cabin fever, or Stockholm syndrome like you said...or some damn thing. We're warned about it, in our training."

Adrian restrained his smile. He'd never seen Seth so confounded by his own state of mind. "My dad always used to say that where there are many excuses, there is no single good excuse."

"What is he, Confucius?"

"He's a practising psychologist." Adrian withheld his smile. "You care about her, face it."

The frown on Seth's forehead deepened. "I care about her, yes, and god knows she was good to be around, but I can't afford to get close to a woman the way I did with Lily, not in my line of work. I can't be there for a woman, not the way a man should be." His eyes looked haunted. "It was a mistake to get so heavily involved."

Adrian didn't comment. They both knew it wasn't a mistake.

"What about you," Seth asked, clearly trying to shift the attention away from himself. "You're more her type, you have a stable life and you two had a relationship on the go before we all met. Adrian...you understand her much better than I do."

"True." Adrian smiled, allowing himself that. "But I'm not sure how deeply she feels for me. She cares, but I know for sure she fell in love with you." Adrian couldn't help smiling when Seth stared at him, confused.

"Love?"

"Yes, love. It was obvious to me after the first two days, but when that bloke Lavonne had her." He shook his head, remembering the intensity of the moment. "The affection you have for her was pretty darn obvious. Face it Seth, you want her, and she wants you."

Seth's eyes flickered. He shook his head. "But you—"

"But me what? I care about her too, a lot. Don't get me wrong, I love the woman."

"Go after her then," Seth said.

"It wouldn't be the same without you, I'm not stupid. The three of us had an amazing experience. There was a symbiosis that I've never found, or seen, and I'd be happy to settle down with a woman like Lily." He paused, ready for the hard part, the part that had kept him awake these past nights. "But if it's you she wants then I'm not going to stop that from happening…neither am I going to let you walk away from her. I know you're about to do just that."

Seth rested his head back against the armchair he was sitting in front of. "I have to walk away. I gave up all rights to a relationship when I went in to this job. It's too hard to maintain a normal relationship." He rubbed his hand over his face and head, scrubbing his hair, before he continued. "I'm away for days and weeks as time. I don't want a woman like Lily worrying about me. It's bad enough that my mother has sleepless nights."

Adrian toyed with the knight in his hand. "Perhaps fate brought us three together."

Seth considered that silently.

Adrian knew he was breaking through. He had two more days, and he would continue to steadily drip feed the idea during that time. He needed Seth to be ready when the moment came. Personally, he'd jump at the chance to be with Lily some more. He'd been part of something special, and he knew it. He wanted to see what happened next. Seth was more stubborn. If it was Seth that Lily really wanted, then he wasn't going to let Seth mess that up. "When we get out of this and the court case is behind us, you have to go see her, we both do."

"I can't."

Adrian could see it there in his friend's eyes, the denial, and the desperately unhappy look. He'd been right. Seth was fighting it, but only because of who and what he was.

"You can, and I'm going to make sure you do." When Seth looked at him, querying, Adrian laughed softly. "It's only fair. I've spent the last two weeks doing as you say, it's about time you listened to me and took my advice."

"And what if it's you that she wants to be with, after all this?" Seth said, a faraway, thoughtful expression in his eyes.

Adrian smiled to himself but didn't respond directly, simply shrugging. It was all he needed to know, because that comment had proved that Seth *did* want her and that deep down he had his own fears, whether he admitted them or not.

They both did.

Fate would decide how this panned out.

Fate, and Lily.

* * * *

Lily sighed and put down the newspaper she'd been reading during her coffee break. For days she'd been scouring the papers for information about court hearings, even though she didn't quite know what she was looking for. She'd heard the name Carlisle, and drug running had been mentioned, but neither of them had said any more about the court case than that. She wasn't sure she wanted to know more, especially after her second run in with Emery Lavonne.

What she *did* need to know was how they both were, because she cared so much it hurt. *I'm in love with them.* Admitting that to herself only seemed to make it worse, like she had a claim, which reinforced the nagging need to know if they were okay and happy. She couldn't get them out of her mind, and often found herself replaying the outrageous things she'd found herself doing, things she had only ever fantasised about before she was thrown together with Adrian and Seth. Every night she slept in the sweatshirt she'd been wearing when the police arrived, the one that both men had worn. Stroking it over her body, she imagined it was them, imagined that they were close against her and she could hold them and love them. Did they think about her at all?

"Are you okay?" It was Andrea, and she'd stuck her head into the storeroom where Lily was perched on a stool, deep in thought. The area at the back of the shop counter was where they took their coffee breaks and kept the stock, and several times since her return Lily had lost track of time in there when her thoughts and emotions had consumed her.

Lily looked wistfully at her friend, who'd been told most — but not all — of the story. "Sorry, I drifted. Are we getting busy?" She nodded out into the shop counter area while she folded the newspaper and shoved it into a drawer.

"We will be soon."

Lily nodded, giving her friend a smile to reassure her. She put her apron back on and pulled her Sandwich Boutique baseball cap to a jaunty angle, and then headed out, taking over from Andrea at the orders end of the counter. They had a part-time worker on the till for when they were at the busiest, and the rush was already on for lunchtime take outs. Lily took a deep breath and got stuck in.

The work made it easier, because the time went more quickly as she wrote down each order and put it together. As usual she tried to chat briefly with each customer before she passed them down the line. Occasionally her mind would drift and she had to force herself to concentrate on getting the orders right. Towards the end of the lunch rush she messed up and toasted a wrap that was ordered straight up. Luckily it was a regular customer who didn't complain too loudly. "I'm so sorry. Your lunch is on the house today."

Picking up her pen, she scribbled on the pad and got ready for the next customer. "What can I get for you today?" she asked when the next customer arrived in front of her.

After a pause, the customer spoke. "Can I get a really basic cheese and pickle sandwich, the boring type?"

She knew that voice — that delicious accent — knew it in a way that stirred her senses and made her heart leap. *Seth*. Faltering, she dropped her pen and her fingers splayed as she steadied herself on the countertop.

"And can we get that with a side order of something a bit more exotic? Whatever you suggest, Lily."

She knew that voice too. *Adrian*.

Staring at them in disbelief, she put her hand to her chest as she looked from one to the other and back again. Then Adrian smiled her way, and she noticed that he'd had a haircut. For court, she realised. They'd been to court already. It was over.

Relief flooded through her.

He'd lost weight too, but he looked happy. Seth, on the other hand, looked as if he had the weight of the world on his shoulders. His hair had grown and his eyes were dark with concern as he looked at her.

"You came to see me." Staring at them both, she wanted to grab them in case they vanished again. "Is it all done, the case?" She directed the question to Adrian.

He nodded, blinking slowly, like a relaxed tomcat. There was a definite change in him, one for the better. That brought about such a rush of emotion that her eyes misted. Her hand went to her mouth. "Oh dear," she said, on the verge of tears.

"Perhaps you'd better take this particular order into the backroom." It was Andrea, and while she spoke she eyed the two men with curiosity. She'd obviously gathered these two were Lily's mystery men.

When the words sank in Lily nodded, thanking her friend and waving the two of them along the counter and behind it, leading the way into the storeroom. There, in that small space, the two men stared at her, expectantly.

It was Adrian who spoke first. "You're a sight for sore eyes, my lovely *Laidbacklady*." He cupped her face in both hands and kissed her on the mouth.

Lily melted into him and rested a hand on his chest, her other hand instinctively reaching for Seth who still hovered by the door. There was tension in him and she silently begged him to touch her.

When she felt his fingers grasp hers and he moved closer, she turned her face towards him. "So good to see you both."

"We couldn't keep away," Seth said, and he gave her that devastating smile of his, the one that she'd missed so badly, even though it had infuriated her so many times.

Adrian's hand was on her back, stroking her, and when she hugged Seth, he held her ever so tightly for a moment and then released her, as if he wasn't sure she wanted to be held. She sensed awkwardness in him and wanted to make it disappear, wanting him to look as relaxed with this reunion as Adrian did.

She wiped her eyes quickly, hoping they hadn't noticed. "Thank you for coming. I've been so worried, and I've missed you both so much."

"Hey, nothing to thank us for." Seth meshed his fingers with hers, and when he did she held his hand tightly against her, afraid he was about to say goodbye and leave.

Adrian grinned, and then gave a quick sidelong glance at Seth, who nodded back at him. Seth cleared his throat. "We were talking, while we were waiting for the case to be heard, and we were kind of wondering," he frowned, "that is, if you aren't seeing anyone else at the moment?"

She shook her head emphatically.

His frown lifted somewhat. "Would you like to go out with one of us, for a proper date?"

Lily stared from one to the other of them, unsure what this meant. "With one of you? Is this like…an ultimatum?"

Adrian put his hand on Seth's shoulder and squeezed it, taking over. Seth looked relieved. "What Seth is trying to say is that we both want to see you again, but we know that you might not want to do that, not now you're back in your normal life. Things were special back there in Wales, and we both know that. It's up to you though, Lily. If you only want to see one of us, we've agreed that the other one will take it on the chin and bow out quietly."

Her breath felt trapped in her lungs, her chest tight and her heart beating wildly. "What if I want to see both of you again?"

It was a risk. Perhaps they wanted her to choose one or the other, but she couldn't do that.

Adrian's smile grew.

Seth's eyes were filled with hope, but his eyebrows were still drawn together. "Thing is, I want to see you again, real bad. But I can't be there all the time for you like Adrian can, not in my line of work. You'd have to say you'd accept that, up front."

She could see how hard this was for him, and as she considered her response she drew his hand to her lips, kissing it gently. "I understand that."

They closed in, both of them, enfolding her. She shut her eyes, savouring that feeling of being surrounded by them, of being loved by them both, wanting them both.

"You're sure?" Seth whispered against her ear, as he kissed her cheek.

The arrogant policeman who needed to be reassured.

Adrian squeezed her bottom, making her smile.

The sensitive accountant, who didn't need to ask.

Deep in her heart, she'd always known that this was truly inescapable. She nodded at them both, her emotions soaring. "I'm sure, very sure."

About the Author

I'm British by birth, but because of my parent's nomadic tendencies I grew up travelling the globe—an only child with a serious book habit. I dreamed of being a writer since the age of 12 and finally began writing seriously in the late 1990s. By that time I'd got myself a BA in Art History, a Masters in Literature and the Visual Arts, and I'd worked in all manner of diverse careers—but the stories in my head simply had to be written.

My first erotic short story was published by Virgin publishing's Black Lace imprint in '97 and things really took off from there. Every spare moment was spent on the stories that bubbled away in my imagination. I've now had work published in over forty anthologies, including Best Women's Erotica, The Mammoth Book of Best New Erotica and the Black Lace Wicked Words series. It was such a thrill for me to find that readers enjoyed my stories. I started working on longer projects around 2003, and I've had novels and novellas published by US publishers Red Sage, Penguin Heat, and the Juno Books fantasy line. I'm very happy to join the team at Total-e-Bound.

Nowadays I live in the north of England—close to the beautiful, windswept landscape of the Yorkshire moors—with my real life hero, Mark. Mark supports my work through all its ups and downs, and somehow manages to keep me sane and grounded when fiction threatens to take over.

Saskia loves to hear from readers. You can find her contact information, website details and author profile page at http://www.total-e-bound.com.

Total-E-Bound Publishing

www.total-e-bound.com

Take a look at our exciting range of literagasmic™
erotic romance titles and discover pure quality
at Total-E-Bound.

Made in the USA
Lexington, KY
31 May 2011